the
ghost
clause

the

ghost
clause

HOWARD NORMAN

Houghton Mifflin Harcourt
Boston   New York
2019

For information about permission to reproduce selections
from this book, write to trade.permissions@hmco.com or to
Permissions, Houghton Mifflin Harcourt Publishing Company,
3 Park Avenue, 19th Floor, New York, New York 10016.

hmhco.com

Library of Congress Cataloging-in-Publication Data
Names: Norman, Howard A., author.
Title: The ghost clause / Howard Norman.
Description: Boston ; New York : Houghton Mifflin Harcourt, 2019. |
Identifiers: LCCN 2018036020 (print) | LCCN 2018038075 (ebook) |
ISBN 9780544988064 (ebook) | ISBN 9780544987296 (hardcover)
Subjects: | BISAC: FICTION / Literary. | FICTION / Family Life. |
FICTION / Occult & Supernatural.
Classification: LCC PR9199.3.N564 (ebook) |
LCC PR9199.3.N564 G48 2019 (print) | DDC 813/.54 — dc23
LC record available at https://lccn.loc.gov/2018036020

Book design by Emily Snyder

Printed in the United States of America

DOC 10 9 8 7 6 5 4 3 2 1

The author is grateful for permission to reprint "Once Later" by
W. S. Merwin, collected in *Garden Time.* Copyright © 2016 by W. S. Merwin,
used by permission of The Wylie Agency, LLC, and Copper Canyon Press.

For Emma and Jane

Once Later

It is not until later
that you have to be young

it is one of the things
you meant to do later

but by then there is
someone else living there

with the shades rolled down
how could you have been young there

at that time
with all that was expected

then what happened to
the expectations

there is no sign of them there
a shadow passes across the window
shade

what do they know in there
whoever they are

—— W. S. MERWIN

the
ghost
clause

MOTION
IN LIBRARY

ZACHARY KNEW from her slightly lopsided smile, eyes squinted tight against tears as she stepped from the farmhouse porch, that Muriel's dissertation defense had been strenuous. Muriel sometimes put her emotions on highest exhibit by exaggerating a suppression of them. "I got through it," she said.

"Oh, I know you did more than that," Zachary said. "Congratulations. You've worked so hard." They had a good kiss. Anyway, she was now Dr. Muriel Streuth. He could also see that the drive in early-December sleet and on icy roads, from Medford, Massachusetts, home to their farmhouse in Calais, Vermont, had worn Muriel to a frazzle.

"How do you want to celebrate?" he asked.

Muriel removed her coat and draped it over a chair. "For starters," she said, "a cup of tea in the bath."

She kicked off her boots, crossed her arms, and, grasping its bottom hem, lifted off her sweater, which she carried into the library. She set her sweater on the rocking chair. She then walked along the wide wooden slats to the first-floor bathroom. She ran a hot bath. Japanese bath salts tinged the water an orange hue. She smiled at the sound of the Chopin nocturne Zachary placed on the old-school phonograph in the living room; they had quite a collection of vinyl albums. The nocturnes were what she often played, arriving home after the long drive, needing just to unwind and not think. Standing in the bathroom doorway, her peach-colored blouse half unbuttoned, her gray slacks on the floor, Muriel called toward the kitchen, "Zach, I only didn't hug and squeeze you because I want to save every ounce of strength for later."

In a few moments, Zachary set a steaming cup of cinnamon tea on the windowsill next to the bathtub. Muriel had been sitting on the rim, one hand monitoring the water level and temperature. She stood and turned off the faucet. She dropped her blouse, brassiere, panties, and socks to the floor, then slid into the bath.

"What a day for you," Zachary said.

He picked up her clothes, carried them to the laundry room, and set them on top of the washing machine. Muriel's clothes could wait. I knew that the volume of bath water, combined with what the wash cycle required, might strain the capacities of the artesian well. Probably not, but why risk an automatic shutdown of the pump, which was at 230 feet. The laundry room window displayed ostrich feathers of frost. Zachary went upstairs.

Watching Muriel and Zachary since I'd died and returned to this farmhouse, I have come to believe that certain evenings delivered them into each other's arms, as if the passing hours themselves had it in mind all day. There was so much human urgency, but also something more, perhaps indefinable. At least I couldn't define it. There just seemed a powerful sense of predestination about it. I'm sure that neither of them would be caught dead using the words "delivered them into each other's arms." That's perhaps my own literary pretention at work. Muriel Streuth and Zachary Anders now own this 1845 farmhouse. Notice I did not say *my former* farmhouse. I am still in residence here. Things should be stated directly, don't you think?

At the age of forty-eight, I died of a heart attack, an hour out to sea, on May 23, 1994, at the rail of the Bar Harbor, Maine–Yarmouth, Nova Scotia, ferry.

Now I must also mention MOTION IN LIBRARY. Muriel and Zachary had put in a state-of-the-art alarm system. There had been some robberies in the neighboring villages of Woodbury and Plainfield. Along with motion detectors, this system included highly sensitive smoke and carbon monoxide detectors. Since I wander freely through the farmhouse, there seemed no determinable logic as to why only the motion detector in the library kept registering a disturbance. It was occurring quite often. I figured it might somehow be a reaction to the metaphysics, or physics, or something, of my condition, and though I don't unfailingly set off the MOTION IN LIBRARY alarm each time I enter the library when the alarm is set, when it does happen, a dispatcher at Onion River Security in Montpelier receives the MOTION IN LIBRARY signal. According to procedure, volunteer responders, in a predetermined order, are telephoned. The way Muriel and Zachary have it, first on the list are Jody and David, writers and translators, who live just around the curve of the dirt road. They are followed by Eric and Cathy, who both work in ecological conservation, then Erica, a radio programmer and private investigator, who lives halfway between the farmhouse and Route 14. Last to be contacted is Jasper Sohms, a retired high school math teacher, who lives in Plainfield. This MOTION IN LIBRARY phenomenon is driving Muriel and Zachary a little bonkers; they are embarrassed to have to keep apologizing to neighbors whom they are only just getting to know. "No big deal," Cathy said. "We do for each other."

When Muriel finally said to Zachary, "Why don't we carry out an experiment and disconnect the motion detector in the library and see what happens?" he said, "Muriel, you want to disconnect the motion detector in the one room motion is being detected? That's counterintuitive." "Counter to your intuition," she said, "but not to anyone else's in the whole world."

This did not amount to a quarrel, only an exchange of sentences with tones calibrated, as Buddhists suggest, to not bring something to a painful point. So far in their two-year marriage, they have been talented at this.

Each time MOTION IN LIBRARY lights up the switchboard, so to speak, it's usually been the first responder located at home who walks or drives over and checks things out. Should none of the responders be home, messages are left, and the volunteer fire department, as a kind of last resort, is called. It costs $145 for them to come out to the house, no matter what they find or don't find.

One time, when none of the first responders could be contacted, Eddie Zeifert, a technician at Onion River Security, met five men from the volunteer fire department at the house, wherein he discovered the 534-page *Collected Poems of Wallace Stevens* open facedown on the library floor. When the next day Eddie stood in the kitchen consulting with Muriel, he'd said, "Mrs. Anders, with that book? Let me put it this way. That book would've had to fly around the room, descend in slow motion, then, at the last possible second, double its weight and rate of speed, and slam to the floor directly on one of the sensors beneath the Turkish rug. Then that MOTION IN LIBRARY alarm might've possibly been set off."

"Thank you for your hypothesis, Edward," Muriel had said. She wrote him out a check for $45, the minimum for a consultation.

Muriel and Zachary's Maine coon cat, named Epilogue (for the fact that he concludes the lives of so many mice), who weighs around sixteen pounds, doesn't usually enter the library unless Muriel is clacking away on her Royal manual typewriter on her desk. And if Muriel is home, the alarm is turned off. In fact, Epilogue likes to drape himself across the typewriter itself. "He's my welcome writer's block," Muriel often said.

Anyway, I feel pretty bad, because, on that aforementioned night, when Muriel and Zachary were at the Savoy Theater in town, dinner afterward, I had indeed been reading *The Collected Poems of Wallace Stevens* when I'd dozed off in the rocking chair, and the book had fallen to the floor, and I fell right on top of it, and slept on the floor. I didn't think I still had weight, and may in fact not weigh anything at all. What woke me was Jasper Sohms saying out loud to himself, "All the goddamn way over here and nothing. Well, maybe there's something in the fridge." I stood up and leaned against a bookshelf. He put *The Collected Poems of Wallace Stevens* on Muriel's desk, then went into the kitchen, where he prepared a Swiss cheese sandwich, and left a note: *The* MOTION IN LIBRARY *went off again. I made a Swiss cheese sandwich. Jasper.*

I've studied it, and there's nothing in the user's manual that could explain what happens here. On yet another occasion, a technician named Abner Frame said, "These old houses have their secrets, is how I like to think of it. There was a house over in Cabot I inspected top to bottom, bottom to top. It could've been anything set their alarm off. A drop of rain blown through a screen door. A spider getting electrocuted. Who knows? My boss likes to say some old farmhouses like yours, they resist anything to do with modern life, and by that he generally means since the Civil War."

If you consider, as I do, an old house as a sentient being that gets into moods and does things on its own volition, then perhaps it's not me setting off the alarm in the first place. Still, I think I should experiment, and stay out of the library when the alarm is set. Problem there is, to me the library is the most comfortable room in the house; it's where all the best books are.

I thought of turning off the alarm itself until I saw headlights in the trees or heard the car coming up the road. But here's what occurred a few days ago when I tried that. Muriel and Zachary had driven over to their new friend Tobin's house for dinner on Jack Hill Road. The moment their car was out of view, I pressed the code to disconnect the alarm, then went into the library. Epilogue sensed something and sauntered in, finally hopping up onto Muriel's desk, then lying across her typewriter, where he closed his eyes. Before I died, I'd decided to reread all the novels of Thomas Hardy. Now, I took *Far from the Madding Crowd* down from the shelf, sat in the rocking chair, and began to read. Reaching page 108, I dozed off. Sudden bouts of sleep happened often to me, night and day. I woke to hear Muriel in the kitchen: "I definitely set the alarm, Zach. You know how compulsive I am about it. You know how afraid of a house fire I am. And you know I run through my mental checklist. I absolutely, positively set the alarm."

"I'll look through the house," Zachary said.

He went into every room, even down to the basement. Muriel stayed in the kitchen. Back at the top of the basement stairs, Zachary said, "It has to be an electronic glitch of some sort. I'll stop by the alarm company tomorrow."

Which he did. Again the company sent out Eddie Zeifert, who checked the entire system and found nothing wrong. The bill this time was $75, for the thorough inspection. Handing a check to Eddie, Muriel said, "Mr. Zeifert, I set the alarm."

BACK TO THE EVENING following Muriel's dissertation defense. It was now snowing heavily. Muriel did not give a thought to putting on her robe after stepping from the bath. Chopin's Nocturne in E-flat Major was playing as she walked up the stairs. Zachary was waiting for her in bed, wearing only a T-shirt with a caricature of Bob Dylan on it and the words HOW DOES IT FEEL? She took a sip from the shot glass of whiskey Zachary had placed on the bedside table. There was dim snow-light, as if delivered from the blanketed field in back of the house, seemingly held by the wide picture window. The bedroom was still warm, but its woodstove was down to glowing embers. Otherwise, the farmhouse was dark. Under the bedclothes Muriel pressed up against Zachary, kissed his ear, whispered sweet nothings, and things began.

This is where I perhaps should have provided myself with an admonition. Counsel, advice, definite reproof, caution — all of these, all of these — and yet I stayed and watched. Things should be stated directly, and while it may not reflect well on me, almost right away when Muriel and Zachary had finished making love, I went up to my cabin to try to find the language to describe what I had seen. I write in longhand in black Moleskine notebooks, which I keep under a pair of loose slats in the floor of my cabin, which is about fifty yards from the house. I fill these notebooks with all sorts of daily observations. Muriel and Zachary may discover them someday and know something of who they were or are, at least by my lights. That sentiment, of course, contains the presumptuousness of any chronicler of another's life. Naturally, I have no antecedent experiences or models for any of this, except possibly the novels of Junichiro Tanizaki, which I read during the last year of my life. There was *The Key* and *Diary of a Mad Old Man,* which are, you might say, imbued with voyeurism and other questionable behaviors, and yet often the unscrupulous and despairing intellects of their first-person narrators demonstrate a hard-earned pathos and, toward marriage itself, an abiding sense of astonishment and melancholy. And I confess to being surprised by and definitely rapt with attention toward Muriel's expertise in Japanese writers bold in their erotic investigations.

The heart is seldom rational — the mind, sometimes.

An hour earlier, Muriel was lying on top of Zachary and had just drawn her husband inside her, a duet of intake of breath and moan, when he said, "What is it? You have a look. What is it?" Muriel held Zachary's arms above his head, situating herself so that she could move her hips ever so slowly, then she took one of his hands and placed it on her lower back. He put his other hand flat against Muriel's heart and said, "Just tell me." "In a moment, in a moment," she said, and closed her eyes. Zachary put his hand on her shoulder while his other hand remained on her back, and Muriel kissed him deeply as they locked into their tight circular motion. Zachary had an expression, as I read it, of hope that his wife would not answer his question, that they would stay lost, away from words.

Muriel's dissertation at Tufts was titled *Parentheses: Poems of Mukei Korin (1890–1941)*. The title referred to Korin's signature invention (considered "modernist") of composing a single line within parentheses, a line that offered an autonomous erotic tableau, yet still interacted with the poem in its narrative entirety. Muriel had translated forty-five of Korin's poems with the help of a friend, Kazumi Tanaka, whom she had originally met at a conference, and who had arranged for her adjunct teaching position on Kazumi's own campus, the University of New Hampshire. Kazumi had provided rough literal renditions in English, which Muriel worked long hours to shape into lines of verse. Muriel had most of them memorized as well. So that when Zachary said again, "Just tell me," she held his face in her hands, caught her breath, and recited:

> Today I feel like a butterfly
> that has landed on an ancient wooden ship.
> I am comfortable in my dimensions.
> I do not feel small or reduced (while traveling the length of her body, he
>   discovers honey with his tongue).
> No one on the ship notices my beautiful wings,
> nor that I am sad.
> All of this is just the way life is.

I had read that very poem on Muriel's desk. And when she recited it to her husband, I felt she was confessing what she wanted, which was to linger awhile inside the parentheses. To ask that Zachary somehow be instructed by what was written there. So when she repeated the line "while traveling the length of her body, he discovers honey with his tongue," Muriel lifted herself from Zachary and lay on her back beside him. Given the parentheses and Muriel's languorous stretched posture then, it was impossible to imagine how the invitation could be misinterpreted. Zachary began to travel with his mouth along her neck, shoulders, then to her breasts, then down along her thigh, and then upward from her knees. It was a far more beautifully complicated moment than I'm able to describe, except to say that it all seemed the best possible use of scholarship. I was happy for them, perhaps even envious, in their marriage, that there were at least forty-four more poems to go, and of course, once memorized, any single poem could be repeated as the occasion demanded.

Zachary was in his fourth month of working on the case of Corrine Moore, a missing child. It was his case, but his agency, the Green Mountain Agency, routinely discussed each case at meetings, held twice a week at least. The agency consisted of the director, David Vlamick, and five investigators, of whom Zachary was the newest. Following protocol, he shared everything he learned in the course of his investigation with law enforcement organizations.

The morning following Muriel's dissertation defense, Zachary startled awake in a cold sweat at 4 a.m. and got right out of bed, drank a glass of water, put on his cotton robe, and got the fire cranked up in the bedroom woodstove. He went into the smaller of two guest rooms, which served as his office. He had copies of the ongoing file on Corrine Moore on his desk. He switched on the gooseneck lamp and sat at his desk, looking at a photograph of Corrine taken a few weeks before she went missing. Sweet-looking kid, she was standing in her family's kitchen holding the *Peterson Field Guide to Moths.* She was wearing khaki shorts and a lime-green T-shirt that read TOO MANY BOOKS, TOO LITTLE TIME, which her mother had purchased at Bear Pond Books in town. She wore black, low-cut tennis shoes. Her dark brown hair was cut short, with a straight line of bangs across her forehead. She had a polka-dot Band-Aid on her right knee. Corrine had a big smile. She was pointing to a moth on the wall, which was quite visible in the photograph. The date written on the back of the photograph was August 19, 1994, only thirteen days before she went missing.

In a short while, Muriel reached for her husband and saw that he wasn't there. She got out of bed and walked to his office. She wore one of Zachary's flannel shirts, nothing else. Standing in the doorway, she said, "Is all that paperwork about Corrine Moore?"

"Yeah, couldn't sleep, so I'm reviewing her file again," he said. "I had a dream of her taking moths from her neighbors' wall. Dream or no, I even recognized which house. It was the McFarlands' on Pine Hill Road. I recognized the chandelier the blacksmith, Bronstein, made for them. I recognized the view through their kitchen window, out to their apple trees. The gazebo."

"You're getting to know where we live in a way most people wouldn't, darling."

"I guess that's right."

She massaged his shoulders. "Only a few steps from us in bed to your desk, for the search for that poor child to begin again. That makes me feel very much in it with you." When she saw that Zachary may have taken this in part as an admonition, or even a statement about the uncomfortably close proximity between joy and sadness, she added, "I think about her a lot, too, my love. I want you to know that. I hope as much as anyone that she's not only alive, but somehow completely unharmed."

"I know," Zachary said. "I know you do."

Muriel went downstairs to the library and typed up a final version of her and Kazumi Tanaka's most recent translation:

Tragedies befall us one after the next,
each more difficult to recover from.

Still, the light this morning was beautiful
in the distant pines, and close by, light was
beautiful in the willow (it's now just dusk, yet with your placing lemon-
   tasting fingerprints on your breasts for me to erase, the folding of
   clothes and making of tea will need to wait).
Friends named their daughter after an actress
who drowned.
Eventually the daughter won every swim
competition — her nickname was Flying Fish.
The morning light is again beautiful.
Today a tragedy may befall us.

Reeling the page out of the typewriter, Muriel carried it upstairs. How long would Zachary be poring over Corrine Moore's file? However, one thing I believed Muriel had learned for certain about her marriage was that, once she determined her husband's mood, she didn't expediently judge it and try right then to change it, but made the effort to put whatever mood he was in to good use. And I believed she wanted Zachary to act likewise toward her.

She went into the kitchen, placed a lemon on the bread board, and cut it in half. She carried the lemon halves up to their bedroom and set them on the bedside table. Outside, it was still steadily snowing. She took off the flannel shirt and folded it on the bureau. In bed again, she read aloud the lines within the parentheses again. She moved the lemon halves a little closer on the table. Seeming drowsy, she waited for Zachary to extricate himself from the ghastly predicament of the missing child, on whom so much depended.

But as it turned out, he kept to his office. He reviewed the complete dossier and took notes. Muriel fell asleep. Zachary brought her a cup of coffee at 8:30 a.m. "Let's go to Kismet for dinner tonight. To celebrate your triumph, Dr. Streuth." She pushed a stack of paperbacks in front of the slices of lemon. "That'd be nice," she said.

He was fully dressed now, jeans, T-shirt, sweater, and thick socks, and held a file folder.

CORRINE
WENT MISSING

ORRINE MOORE went missing on September 1, 1994. She
was last seen by Virginia Thomas at about 10:30 a.m.,
when Corrine had walked into the Adamant village co-op
and purchased two apples with the exact change. After Virginia rang up the purchase on the old hippopotamus cash register, as the staff at the co-op called it, Corrine said she was off to feed the apples to some horses in a nearby field. "Corrine had her satchel with her like always," Virginia told Zachary. "Everything seemed just peachy."

Every newspaper in Vermont had picked up the police dispatch, and the very next day, on Vermont Public Radio's *Vermont Edition,* the entire program was devoted to the general phenomenon of missing children. A MISSING CHILD (as opposed to a MISSING PERSON) poster, with Corrine's photograph, appeared in post offices statewide. Within a week, Corrine's parents, Johanna and Devon, had thumbtacked their own personalized poster, which included a collage of recent photographs of their daughter, on bulletin boards —or taped them to the windows—of dozens of general stores, as far-flung south as Bennington, east to the New Hampshire border, west along Lake Champlain, and north to the Canadian border. Of course, US and Canadian border-crossing officers had a photograph and information about Corrine. I suppose there was a kind of homegrown optimism there, that somehow Corrine was still in Vermont. Besides, what more could Johanna and Devon do? I overheard Zachary saying that the Moores telephoned the state's Bureau of Criminal Investigation and Department of Public Safety at least once every single day. And they had approached the Green Mountain Agency the same week Corrine went missing. Zachary told Muriel, "Mr. Vlamick took me aside and said, 'A missing child needs your full attention.' When Mr. Vlamick said that, I knew it was the severest understatement I would ever hear in my life."

Town meeting is usually held the first week in March. Yet shortly after Corrine disappeared, Zachary asked the Calais town clerk, Misty Brick—talk about a name that contains opposites!—to call a separate meeting in Town Hall. This took place on September 15. I heard Muriel and Zachary discussing it that night at the kitchen table. The meeting had adjourned at 8:30, and they were having a late dinner: mushroom omelets, salad, and Muriel had made a cherry pie. Cherry pie with vanilla ice cream was their mutual favorite.

"A lot of people showed up," Zachary said. "I'd say at least two hundred. From Adamant, Woodbury, Calais, Cabot, Plainfield, some from Montpelier. Kids were there, too. The fourth-graders at Calais Elementary did color portraits of

Corrine in chalk, and those were hung along the back wall. That was really something to see. And guess who was in attendance? Lorca Pell. I haven't seen her since she sold us this house, come to think of it."

"She visits her husband's grave quite often," Muriel said. "I see her stepping into his cabin, too. Of course, I don't bother her. It's so private when she's up at the grave."

"She sat right up front," Zachary said. "I told her I hoped she'd come by for dinner soon."

"I hope she does, too. I like her a lot. I think she's just biding her time before visiting us. Coming back inside the farmhouse again."

"Makes perfect sense."

"I'm glad you had such good attendance. How'd it go?"

"First, what happened was, Misty Brick introduced me as a new person in Calais. She said that I was married to you — mentioned you by name. 'Muriel is a professor.' Said that I'd been hired by the Green Mountain Agency to lead the private investigation into Corrine Moore's having gone missing. 'It may be a private investigation, but it's everyone's public concern. So many of us here know the Moore family. So many of us here know Corrine.' Basically, what I did was say that I was in constant touch with Johanna and Devon. They weren't there, and I didn't expect them to be. I had my note cards. I talked a little about procedure. Then I said there was a very intense search going on. At which point, Misty Brick, not exactly interrupting, said, 'There's nothing definite yet. I'm sure Zachary, here, is very sorry to report that. All of us are worried as can be. And by the way, a calendar of prayer vigils has been posted. Next one's tomorrow at Lisa and Patrick Flood's house in Woodbury. There will be live music. Bring food.' Misty knew the people there and read the mood perfectly. She spoke for me, and I was grateful."

"Should we go to the prayer vigil?" Muriel asked.

"I don't know."

"What's the pros and cons, do you think?"

"If you go to a prayer vigil, does that demonstrate getting too emotionally attached? But it's a child, so how can you not be attached? I called my boss. His vote was against."

"I think we should go," Muriel said.

"All right, we're going."

Two evenings after the prayer vigil, when Zachary was out working a lead and Muriel had driven to hear a lecture at Dartmouth College on an Edo-period folding screen, *Women Contemplating Folding Fans,* I read through many of the testimonies Zachary had taken from friends and neighbors of Corrine Moore and her family. This was added to what I already knew quite well of Corrine's biography, as Lorca and I were friends with Johanna and Devon and had first met Corrine when she was a week old, at a kind of welcome-to-the-world potluck at the Moores' 1880 farmhouse, set on five acres in Adamant, less than half a mile from the co-op.

Two midwives had helped home-deliver Corrine. Johanna was forty and it had been a difficult labor, and both midwives stayed on to help for a week after the birth. Devon served as an adjunct lecturer in the history of agriculture at Johnson State College and kept a year-round greenhouse in which he grew orchids. His orchid business did pretty well, but the overhead was high, and he had two half-time employees, a man in his late thirties and his wife, who was a couple of years older—these were Frances and Robert Tremain. I had met them but once, briefly, and knew only that they lived in St. Johnsbury. In the file it said that Devon had referred to the Tremains as "quick studies where orchids are concerned, and most of the time assiduous, but also they have a bickering relationship with the world. It's all been manageable so far. Not great shakes but manageable. Sure, I'd rather have PhD's in botany, but can't on my budget."

Johanna taught art classes at St. Johnsbury Academy, grades seven through twelve, which was about a forty-five-minute drive from Adamant, depending on road conditions, especially in winter. She was considered full-time faculty, but her classes met only on Monday, Wednesday, and Friday. Corrine started to be homeschooled by Karen Zauer, the former librarian at Calais Elementary, at age seven. Before that, Johanna often took Corrine to work and hired this or that student to look after her while Johanna held classes, coordinating with a given student's open study periods—what used to be called study hall. Of course, Johanna had taught many of these students, knew that most of their families were economically strapped, and there was never any shortage of trustworthy teenagers to look after Corrine.

Corrine was homeschooled less for philosophical reasons than as the result of a sequence of appointments and conversations the Moore family had had a month after Corrine's sixth birthday. Having observed certain behaviors in their daughter, Johanna and Devon had brought her to Lorca's good friend Alexandra, a child psychologist in Montpelier.

Lorca and I heard all about this at dinner in our farmhouse on a summer's evening years later. "Basically, our daughter doesn't want to do anything but gather moths from our walls and let them go," Johanna had said. "Also, she makes a huge fuss—I mean screaming and tearing her hair out—if first thing in the morning we don't walk her over to a few neighbors' houses so she can lift whichever moths off their walls, too."

"Bring her over here if you want," I said. "We get all sorts, mainly in the living room."

"I don't quite think that's the point," Lorca said.

"You know how it is with moths every summer," Devon said. "And Corrine sort of studies them before she lets them go free."

"How do you mean?" Lorca asked.

"Corrine's ten now, you know," Johanna said. "But—and I don't know if this is the right word for it. She's kind of a savant. Your psychologist friend Alexandra—we'd had a few appointments with her—she calls someone like Corrine an 'autistic savant.' She says that autism isn't all that well documented, but apparently it's everywhere. But all the stuff we don't yet understand aside, the thing is, Corrine has become a kind of—"

"Lepidopterist," Devon said. "It's incredible, really. She's way below average in every way other kids her age are, that's what the tests showed."

"We didn't know about any tests," Lorca said.

"We've kept it private until we sat down with you just now," Devon said.

"Corrine has all but memorized the *Peterson Field Guide to Moths,*" Devon said, "a book she sleeps with, let alone carries everywhere. I mean, for goodness' sake, she knows all the Latin names. I kid you not. Take a gander at this—"

Johanna set a notebook on the table, opened it, and flipped through the pages, stopping at two drawings of moths done in colored pencil. They clearly were not merely copied out of a field guide. They contained great specificity of color and general physiology, and Corrine had depicted each moth open-winged, in order to reveal its colorful back underwings. She had also jotted down the time of day each moth was plucked from a wall, and whose wall she'd taken it from, and where she had released it. For example, "ANNA TIGER MOTH (*Grammia anna*)—let go at Sodom Pond," written in Corrine's large print. And "HARNESSED TIGER MOTH (*Apantesis phalerata*)."

"Devon and I found two other notebooks like this one," Johanna said. "Page after page of different moths, or the same type of moth on different days, and so forth."

"What do you imagine might happen when it gets cold and there's no moths?" Lorca asked.

Johanna said, "We haven't the slightest idea."

"We asked Corrine what's going on, of course," Devon said. "We try to get her to use her words. She said, 'Do you like that I know so much?' It was heartbreaking. Yes, yes, yes, of course we like it. So Corrine just shrugged—"

"You know," Johanna said, "as if to say, what's the worry, then?"

As the conversation continued, Lorca and I learned that

Alexandra had recommended a specialist in autism named Grete Hoffman, who had a private practice in Middlebury and also taught child psychology at Skidmore College one semester each year. Dr. Hoffman had agreed to drive to Adamant to observe Corrine.

Dr. Hoffman's report ended up in Zachary's file, and from what I read, Dr. Hoffman had arrived to the Moores' farmhouse on the appointed day at 6:30 a.m., only to discover that Corrine had already lifted eight moths from the living room and kitchen walls, drawn each in a notebook, and let six moths flutter off into the apple trees near the greenhouse. A yellow crocus geometer (*Xanthotype sospeta*) and a white-dotted prominent (*Nadata gibbosa*) had died during the night, so Corrine had pressed those into her notebook.

Devon had then walked with Dr. Hoffman the hundred or so yards down the road to the house of Denise and Oakland Faber. They raised goats and sold goat milk and goat cheese all over the state. Johanna had telephoned ahead, so that when Devon and Dr. Hoffman arrived, Oakland met them on his wide porch. When everyone stepped into the kitchen, the Fabers' young daughter, Miriam, was sitting at the table with Corrine. Corrine was drawing a dead moth, a once-married underwing (*Catocala unijuga*), which lay on the tablecloth next to a bowl of oatmeal with maple syrup and brown sugar, which Miriam had prepared for Corrine. Also on the table: a box of colored pencils, a magnifying glass, and the field guide.

Everyone left Corrine and Dr. Hoffman alone to talk. In about half an hour, the two of them walked to Annie and

Mayhew Dickens's farmhouse. Nobody was at home there, but Corrine didn't hesitate to walk right in. A plate of peanut butter cookies was on the kitchen table. A napkin was next to the plate, and there was an arrow drawn on the napkin, pointing to the cookies. Corrine placed her notebook on the table. Devon and Johanna showed up. Corrine proceeded to carefully lift several moths from the Dickenses' kitchen wall and from a screened window in the pantry. The moths were alive, and she carried them one by one out of the front door. She then sat at the kitchen table, ate a cookie—didn't offer one to Dr. Hoffman—composed new drawings, and wrote things in her notebook. After about forty minutes, she put the field guide, pencils, magnifying glass, and notebook into her cloth book bag and said, "I want to go home."

At Zachary's desk, not only did I read Dr. Hoffman's report, but I paged through Corrine's actual notebook, which illustrated to me that her artistic talent was undeniable. Each moth was drawn with a compelling sense of nuance. Corrine was a child of eleven, a child of minimal comportments, and yet her moths would likely be considered, by any standard I would think, not a child's drawings. Newly added: a chocolate prominent (*Peridea ferruginea*), a decorated owlet (*Pangrapta decoralis*), a lost owlet (*Ledaea perditalis*), an indomitable melipotis (*Melipotis indomita*), a smeared dagger (*Acronicta oblinita*), a figure-seven moth (*Drasteria grandirena*), a false underwing (*Allotria elonympha*), a girlfriend underwing (*Catocala amica*), and two black zigzags (*Panthea acronyctoides*).

I saw headlights against the trees. I placed Corrine's notebook exactly where I'd found it. I heard the entrance alarm,

then the OFF code being activated. Then Zachary walked upstairs to his office. He slumped into his swivel chair, took up
a small tape recorder, and began to talk:

"October first. I followed up on a possible sighting of Corrine Moore. A Mrs. Beverly Lowdenstall reported seeing
Corrine 'in the company of religious types' — her words
on the phone recording. I drove to the home of Beverly
Lowdenstall on Maple Hill in Plainfield, and spoke to her for
about half an hour. Of course I took notes. BL said that late
afternoon yesterday she was walking past Country Books in
Plainfield when an 'old wreck of a car' pulled up in front of
the hardware store across the street. Since BL was walking
to Maple Valley Country Store on Route 2 to buy a birthday card for her cousin, she had to walk past the hardware.
She said that when she reached where the 'suspicious old
car' was parked and idling, the driver got out and went into
the hardware store. I quote: 'He looked exactly like Rasputin
— thin gaunt face, dark menacing eyes, long scraggly black
beard, and he wore a black greatcoat, and dangling from
around his neck was a heavy jeweled cross. And it wasn't just
a cross, but Jesus was on it, too. And the funny thing was,
the Jesus highly resembled this Rasputin.' When I asked BL
how she even knew what Rasputin looked like, she said — I
quote — 'From the movie.' I suggested the title was *Nicholas and Alexandra,* and she said, 'Yes, that's the one! The man
who went into the hardware was the spitting image of Rasputin in that movie.' I suppose I should look up publicity
shots from *Nicholas and Alexandra.* I can ask Rick Winston, the
owner of the Savoy Theater, maybe to help me out with this.
He's a recent friend and seems a very honest, straightforward

fellow, and from what I heard knows everything there is to know about movies.

"Following the interview, I drove with BL to the hardware store in Plainfield village proper. When we were standing in front of the store, BL said—this is directly from my notes—'I looked into the car. Another religious-type man was in the passenger-side front seat, and in the back seat was a woman eating an ice cream sandwich. She had on a black dress, way too heavy for this time of year. Her hair was tied up in a bun and she had a mean face, and when she saw me she tried to look not-mean and failed. I wasn't fooled for a second. And that's when I saw little Corrine Moore. She was also eating an ice cream sandwich. And she was wearing a heavy black dress, too. Like I said, too heavy for the season.' When I showed BL a photograph of Corrine and asked if she was absolutely certain it was the same girl, she said, 'If you do a lineup, if you let me look through the one-way window, and you get five girls Corrine's age standing there, each wearing a heavy black dress—and maybe you'd want to give each of them an ice cream sandwich—I'd pick Corrine out in a split second.' I simply thanked BL and drove her home, and then drove back to the Green Mountain Agency office, where I Xeroxed all of my notes and such.

"So, okay, I'll be sharing all of this with every other agency I'm obligated to, but here's my preliminary assessment: BL is a singularly dubious witness. First of all, what she said about a police lineup, that's a complete hero fantasy or something like that. Second, BL couldn't even differentiate between victim and perpetrator. You don't put victims in a lineup. I guess it never occurred to BL that if we were to put Corrine in a lineup, it meant we had already located her and would be jumping for joy. My best guess is that BL is off her rocker. Still, all leads have to be followed up on. So tomorrow I'll go interview the owner of the Plainfield hardware, and see what's up there. I doubt anything. Frustrated, frustrated, frustrated, and this may still be very early days. Corrine went missing on September first — that's a month of pure torment for Johanna and Devon Moore. I hope not torment in any way, shape, or form for Corrine. Additional stuff to record tomorrow."

On the evening of October 5, Muriel drove directly from her adjunct teaching at the University of New Hampshire in Durham to the Kismet restaurant in Montpelier, where she met Zachary for dinner. When I saw headlights ricocheting across the trees, I punched in the alarm code and stayed out of the library, where for much of the evening I'd been reading *The Mayor of Casterbridge*. Muriel and Zachary went almost immediately up to their bedroom. The folder of Korin's poems wasn't on the bedside table where it often could be found. Muriel sat on the rocking chair and Zachary sat on the four-poster bed and leaned against the headboard. The space between them, it seemed to me, served the same function as a moat.

"You don't seem too happy," Zachary said.

Muriel got up and walked to her bureau, took out a pair of pajamas, walked into the bathroom, closed the door. When she emerged, she was wearing the pajamas. Zachary had stripped off all of his clothes except for a T-shirt with a picture of Jimi Hendrix on it and the words ALL ALONG THE

WATCHTOWER. He was under the bedclothes, which he'd pulled up to his chest. He had the pillows situated so that he could sit straight up.

"I know I'm brooding," Muriel said. "But Zach, why'd you invite your colleague—what's her name?"

"You know her name. Jenine Twombly."

"Your colleague Jenine, why'd you invite her and her husband—"

"Mark."

"—to join us for dinner? When they'd just come over to our table to say hello."

"I saw right away you weren't pleased with that."

"I thought we were going to have a romantic dinner, is the thing."

"I wanted to have a romantic dinner. I don't know why I did what I did."

"Maybe you can figure that out. It kind of ruined the evening for me. Sorry, but it did. I'm very tired now."

"Put-on-your-winter-pajamas tired."

"Who said I always have to be subtle?"

"Not me."

"Anyway, I'm really upset about—you might say *disturbed* —was that the conversation was entirely about Corrine Moore. I shouldn't, not with us, Zach, not here in our bedroom, ever have to tiptoe around a thing, right? But I want to be careful. Because I feel there's suddenly a lot at stake here. And I don't want to sound all selfish and witchy."

"Just tell me. I'm really sorry. Just tell me."

"I get that it's your first case at this new agency. I think

I even get the pressure you're under. I get that you're under the scrutiny not only of your new boss, but the whole new community we live in now. That's a lot. I get that, in a way, you're living with this little girl night and day—that didn't come out quite right. Of course, of course, of course it's hard to separate your professional life from private life. Married life. But I think this little girl's situation, in particular, is tearing you apart, because you're the kind of person to get torn apart by it. I love you all the more for that. It sounds so petty and selfish, Zachary, things I'm not, but it's just that I thought we were going to have one kind of dinner, and I couldn't get a word in edgewise. I mean, three investigators at the same table, and me. It's sounds so—compared to the importance of a missing little girl, I mean. I only wanted to tell you I'd had a kind of breakthrough changing my dissertation into a book, like I've been trying to do. My world of seriousness just wasn't your world of seriousness. I see that now."

"It's so exciting about your book, and I want to hear about that in detail. But for now, I realize I wrecked your evening."

"It was like my actual sympathies were being tested, which I guess is good to think about anyway. I just got blindsided."

"I know it's not the same, but you bring your work home, too, right?"

"The Japanese poems? No, not quite the same, is it? Those poems are supposed to work on our behalf."

There was silence for a few moments. "Well," Muriel said, "everyone says don't go to sleep angry."

"Okay, I'll just go to sleep worried and confused."

"But not angry."

"I'm completely sorry about dinner."

Muriel took a sip of whiskey from the bottle on the shelf of the bedside table. She offered the bottle to Zachary, who shook his head. Muriel got into bed and turned off the bedside lamp. "Notice I didn't button my top button," she said.

THE
ONGOINGNESS

EVERY WAKING MOMENT, I'm astonished that I have any consciousness. I feel like a stenographer of the after-life—what am I to call myself now, a revenant? An apparition? An entity? I need to find a word in any language that might work. I have no useful spiritual predisposition or references. Here's how I often feel I would appear, if I appeared: like that famous hollowed-out-looking man on the bridge in Edvard Munch's *The Scream*. This image keeps recurring to me. What's more, here's a phrase that I am tempted to begin every single sentence with: *In the hours still left.* Because that is what I really feel, that my hours of consciousness, of ongo-ingness, in whatever one might call my present status—I prefer to call it *the ongoingness*—are limited. But by what defi-nition are they limited? Perhaps the afterlife is like starting a new life within the one I had. Like that line from the French poet Paul Éluard I love so much: *There is another world, but it is in this one.* The bardo might come closest, yet that Tibetan phenomenon requires a long journey in which you have to conquer certain demons. But I'm just here in my safe farm-house where I've always been.

I've just today found one library shelf still filled with Lorca's books and a box of recipes written out on three-by-five cards. For some reason, Lorca didn't take these from the house, to keep or give to the Kellogg-Hubbard Library or sell at Country Books. I was absent-mindedly looking at the recipes when I saw one for lemon chicken that I'd been competent at cooking. It brought to mind, with the immediacy of a reel of film, the evening before I'd left on the ferry for Nova Scotia, to do a literary reading and lecture at Dalhousie University. I didn't often get invited to do such things. And as it turned out, it was my final journey, as it were, besides my being returned home for burial.

On an evening before I left for Bar Harbor, I prepared lemon chicken in the Dutch oven. Lorca, beautiful love of my life, we were in the sixteenth year of our marriage, and yet she and I had conversed that evening over dinner with the affected casualness that befitted avoidance, and it wasn't difficult to tell that this made us both separately sad. Lorca got up from the kitchen table, kissed me on the forehead. "I'll put on coffee," I said. Clearing the dinner dishes, she said, "Let's watch *The Letter*, okay? You know, the Bette Davis flick, with the most frightening ending ever."

The movie ended at 11:50. "I've got to finish packing," I said.

I had a twenty-year-old leather duffel. I was laying in it a few shirts, underwear, a pair of Italian wool trousers, dress shoes, sports coat. I was supposed to be away from home for only four days. Lorca sat on the end of our bed. "Want to know my most recent secret?" she asked.

"Of course," I said.

"In my studio, I've watched *The Letter* every afternoon for ten days running."

"I don't understand," I said.

I placed an extra pair of socks in the duffel, along with a copy of the short novel *In the Dutch Mountains* by Cees Nooteboom, a recent favorite author. I then sat in the overstuffed chair.

"Want a shot of your favorite vodka?" she asked.

"From the look on your face, I think I should want one."

Lorca went down to the kitchen, got the bottle of vodka out of the freezer, poured each of us a shot glass, and carried them back. I thought, this is a very difficult time between us. She was deep into her Emily Dickinson–inspired paintings, working longer hours than usual in her studio above the Adamant co-op. I mean a sequence of twenty paintings, more or less inspired by the line *We talked between the rooms.* Once, in the middle of the night, several weeks into this project, Lorca startled awake and said, "I wonder if Emily was barren."

I thought at first Lorca was talking in her sleep, but then she put her hand on my shoulder and said, "Sorry, darling, I'm just muttering in the dark."

I'd always felt that in a marriage, if you hit rough waters, you try not to capsize — I'm a writer but not adverse to such clichés on occasion, especially when a touch desperate — and if the situation puts you in extremis, you try to figure out a way to start a new marriage within the one you already have. However, sitting there that night, after we clinked glasses, such platitudes felt useless. As Chekhov wrote, any given moment can suddenly fill you with a sense of elegiac anticipation. It felt dreadful.

Lorca said, "I'm not going to just sip." She threw back her vodka, let the sting and warmth of it register, flattened her hand against her chest, and said, "Whew! That helps."

"Helps what?"

"Just *helps*, Simon."

"Why put yourself through it? *The Letter.* If the ending so frightens you."

"I guess it's to keep discovering that the ending is worse than I remembered, even just from the afternoon before."

"Bette Davis's guilt, that she's had the affair, becomes her fate, right? She walks into that moon-covered-by-dark-cloud alley and gets stabbed."

"She knows she's walking to her death, that's the thing. I've always thought she knew. It all feels predestined. How did she put it? 'With all my heart, I still love the man I killed.' But you'd be wrong, Simon, if you thought I was having an affair."

"I didn't think that. Why would I ever think that? We have other problems, but not that. Besides, it may be that Bette Davis just lost the will to live."

"Well, there's different theories about that."

"I hate that," I said.

"Hate what?"

"That there's different theories."

"Why?"

"Because it means I may not be right."

"I'm not in a laughing mood, Simon, but that's funny."

"I'll miss you when I'm in Halifax."

This was a wretched impasse. Naturally, I had hoped that Lorca would've immediately returned the sentiment. Offered even an approximation of "I'll miss you, too." But she was incapable of hiding ambivalence, which I did love about her. Nor was she capable of contradicting our recent sense of estrangement. All of the above and perhaps more. Though we slept in the same bed every night, we hadn't made love in five weeks.

"I know you'll miss me," she said. "I know you will."

The previous January, what I came to think of as "the incident at the Adamant co-op" took place. It was a small thing, but in a personal way, it led to big damages. That morning, after my usual 5 a.m. to 9 a.m. work on a novel that was in great disrepair—actually, what I'd mostly been doing was reading the collected letters of Robert Louis Stevenson and the complete letters of Virginia Woolf, with the letters of Hart Crane in the offing—I drove my rattletrap yellow Ford pickup to the co-op. Already, I could almost taste the buttered cranberry scone just out of the co-op's small toaster oven. It sometimes seemed that the colder it was, the earlier on my drive to the co-op I began to taste the scone. And that morning the temperature hovered around ten degrees above. When I arrived, Rick Winston was picking up his mail at the cubbyhole of the P.O., next to the checkout counter and cash register, and we chatted for a moment, each holding a paperboard cup of coffee. Rick recommended that Lorca and I see a film called *I Don't Want to Talk About It,* a drama starring Marcello Mastroianni, playing at the Savoy. I asked if he'd had good attendance, to which he replied, "One night yes, the next no. But I think you and Lorca would like it. Afterward, you could say, 'I don't want to talk about it.'" Rick left the store.

Vanessa Sprague, who was about seventy-five, I would guess, was behind the counter. She lived alone in a cottage nearby on Centre Road. She was tidying up. "Hello, Vanessa," I said. "How are you today?"

She answered, give or take a word, as she had each of the hundreds of times before: "You can see for yourself. I'm older than I was yesterday." In my life in Vermont, everything I loved most happened most every day: village life, I mean, where familiarities become expectations.

"You going upstairs to see Lorca?" she asked. "Oh, I'd get right up there if I was you. She's got Emily Dickinson up there with her again. Shouldn't you step in? What a wimp you are, Simon. She's taking your wife away from you."

"Vanessa, you don't know shit about Lorca's creative inspirations," I said. It already sounded inane, but I continued, in a kind of fugue state of irritability. "She doesn't confide in you, does she? What is it? Do you go upstairs when she's not there and have a look and come to conclusions? You don't know shit about painting, Vanessa. You don't know shit about Emily Dickinson!"

"I seemed to have touched a nerve," she said. "No matter, silly boy. Just be aware that the cranberry scones were just delivered. They're over there next to the cookies. In their usual place."

Lorca was already something of an established painter when I first met her, in early September, 1975, in Providence, where she was a thirty-year-old instructor at her alma mater, the Rhode Island School of Design. She taught two studio art courses. I was subletting a friend's small apartment on Perkins Street. I had about a year's worth of savings from painting houses the previous spring and summer, mainly in Providence, though I had a few houses up in Boston, too. I was twenty-nine at the time, and had already written three novels, each and every one an abject failure, but at least I'd written them. I hadn't been in any creative writing workshops, although I wondered what they might be like. Anyway, I had a new novel going. Nothing particularly special about my writing life. Working on habits of persistence, and working on how to read my own stuff critically, type up twenty pages on the Remington manual, crumple up nineteen. Cross out half of that saved page. How else to go about it? When anyone talks about the aesthetics and arduousness of a writing life — as if it is being forced on them by certain mystical insistences, or maybe a condition of ancient desires, as Robert Graves on Majorca so prodigiously suggested — it all so embarrasses me. Therefore, I feel I've already said too much about my existence in those days; let us please leave it at that.

Near the Perkins Street apartment, I saw a notice on a café window: MODELS WANTED FOR PORTRAIT STUDIO COURSE. I showed up at the designated hour to a room where Lorca was the instructor. Right away, I saw that she left the choice of model up to her students. It was a merciless and comical thumbs-up or thumbs-down selection. The pay was $10 an hour. My funds were running low.

Lorca was dressed in black jeans, flats, and a flannel shirt, over which she wore a paint-spattered dark blue smock, tie-strings dangling at each side. Her auburn hair was pulled back into a ponytail, fastened by a rubber band. She wore light brown, round-rimmed eyeglasses. She was lithe and about my height, which was five foot nine, and she was using crutches. I thought the thickness and, as she spoke, slight rise and fall of her eyebrows endearing, but I admit they provided a brief Groucho Marx moment. She also had a smattering of freckles along either side of her nose and as-tonishingly sensual lips, even when exhibiting what I soon learned was her signature downturned smile. None of this description suffices, really. Love at first sight—well, perhaps not, but certainly curious, and in a matter of a few weeks, devoted to our courtship, closely followed by smitten. At any rate, she saw me notice her crutches and pointed to a young man sitting in a wooden chair, very handsome, very fit, completely nude, who was the object of the students' ar-tistic attentions—that is, their individual charcoal draw-ings. "See that guy there?" she said. "He pushed me out of a train."

I could only shrug and say, "And yet you hired him."

"Jeez, just kidding, you know?" she said. "What really happened was, I sprained my ankle. Methought 'twer broke but 'tweren't a-tall. Are you here because of the notice?"

"Yes," I said.

From my left, I heard a woman's voice: "We drew his body type last week, Lorca." An obviously informal atmosphere, everyone on a first-name basis. "I like his face, sort of—not really." I turned to look and saw two men and two women, sketching side by side at their easels, in a synchronized movement give me a thumbs-down. I turned back to Lorca, who said, "Sorry about that. But look, the guy I live upstairs from said they're looking for a waiter at Finelli's, on Pine Street. In case you're interested."

The next afternoon, I had an interview at Finelli's. The manager looked at my application. "Says here you're twenty-nine. Oh, shit, another starving-artist type or what?"

"Do waiters and waitresses here get meals?"

"One meal per shift. You'd be working nights."

"Then I won't starve, will I."

Lorca was a regular at Finelli's. She usually came in with a faculty colleague or a few students. I waited on her at least a dozen times. I eavesdropped on her conversations. Six or so weeks after I started the job, I found Lorca sitting alone in a corner booth. "Would you like to hear tonight's specials?" I asked. She was dressed in her teaching clothes, pretty much as I'd first seen her, except for a black button-down sweater and a flannel-lined trench coat, which she preferred to keep on. No crutches in sight.

"They're always the same," she said. "Not sure what makes them special anymore."

"Tonight is different. Tonight we have potato-leek soup, and guess what? It's my own recipe. I asked permission of the chef. She tried it out and didn't die."

"Get out," she said. "*Your* recipe?"

"The courtesy of a waiter, the soul of a maker of soup."

"I'm in a 'I hate life' mood, so maybe I should try your soup. They could make for the perfect couple."

"You can first consult with our chef, Lorraine, who looks so much like Bette Davis."

"You know, I think she does, too."

"Early, midcareer, like in *Now, Voyager,*" I said.

"Oh, I get into arguments about that movie."

"With whom?"

"None of your beeswax, Mr. Waiter. And truth be told, I never much liked potato-leek soup."

"Don't order it, then. But if you don't, it'd be an example of the customer not always being right."

"Do you realize what's at stake here?"

"My tip, probably."

"Not probably."

"I've got other tables, but it seems I'm suddenly dedicated to your whims."

"Wait—I know that line. Don't tell me. Definitely spoken by Bette Davis. I can't recall which movie."

"Then you don't know her movies as well as you think you do, Lorca."

"Oh, it's Lorca, now, is it?"

"I just figured, if your students can call you by your first name . . ."

"I'll have a cup of the potato-leek soup. Not a bowl. And the salade Niçoise. And a glass of the house white."

"I hate repartee. I'd rather steal a car and not talk."

"I know that line. Can't remember the exact movie, but Bette didn't have a big part."

I wrote down her order and fastened it to the rotating clips all the orders went on; Lorraine's assistants grabbed them through the open window. When the food was ready to serve, a waiter's individual number was called, "Six— order up!," and the plate set on the counter.

I waited until Lorca was done with her soup and had pushed the cup away. When I set her salad on the table, I could see she looked distraught, but tried to hide it. "Should I call nine-one-one?" I asked.

"Soup was good, actually. You're referring to my sour-puss expression? No, see, they cut me down to one course for next semester. Which means I won't be able to make my rent. Which means I can't pay for canvases for a while, or paint. Which means, forget it, I'm going to splurge. I want you to bring two more glasses of wine, plus two desserts, so bring back the menu, please, so I can choose which two, thanks." She polished off the first glass of wine and handed me the glass. "I hate *La Bohème*," she said. "I mean, I love Puccini. I even saw *Madame Butterfly* in Genoa once. But *La Bohème* I find — I don't know — the starving-artist stuff always gets me anxious about my rent."

"Very practical response." I couldn't help but smile.

"What's so funny? You obviously don't have a trust fund yourself, right?"

"No, sorry. It's just that I had this friend, Daniel — Danny Steiner, Canadian guy, who got a job operating a Zamboni in Vancouver's public ice rink. And the entire repertoire over the loudspeaker was Puccini. He said to me, 'Sometimes I think if I have to listen to *La Bohème* one more time, I might go berserk and slam the Zamboni into the concession stand.'"

"Funny thing, that. I always wanted to marry a Zamboni operator."

"I'll give you Danny's address and phone. Should I write it on a napkin?"

"Oh, a long-distance relationship's not for me. Thanks but no thanks."

I didn't see Lorca for another three months. We next ran into each other at a poetry reading by May Swenson, sponsored by the English Department at Brown University. Or, as Lorca called it, "Snobsville U." I hadn't yet stepped foot on the Brown campus, so didn't know either way. I knew they offered some creative writing workshops, though. May Swenson had just published a new collection, which had a striking jacket illustration of a cockatoo. Strapped for cash or not, I'd so loved her reading that I purchased a copy. I hadn't sat next to Lorca, but after the reading we spoke for a few minutes. We made a date to take a walk, which we did the next week. Hours, we talked about painting and books. "No college for you, right?" she said. "I hope, God forbid, that doesn't make you some sort of arrogant autodidact."

"Nothing other than what I said. Waiter and trying to write a novel. Commonplace résumé, I'm afraid. I failed at a few novels and now hope not to."

"I'm already what I want to be. And so are you. From now on, that's how I prefer to look at it."

After that long walk, we had dinner together. And after that, we were pretty much inseparable.

BUT TO RETURN to the incident at the Adamant co-op: That evening, Lorca and I watched *Dr. Zhivago* on TV, after which she said, "Want some tea?" We sat drinking lemon tea and eating Scottish shortbread cookies. It was snowing steadily. A hammock of moon was traveling pale in hazy light, and here and there stars could be seen in sudden openings of black sky. Lorca said, "I should tell you something, Simon."

"Okay."

"I heard your heated exchange—or whatever it was—with Vanessa this morning."

"Oh, I thought you were upstairs in your studio."

"I was coming down for a coffee," Lorca said.

"Vanessa's a real piece of work."

"You don't know the half of it."

"Well, the half I do know—"

"I probably should've either gone back upstairs or barged right in. Instead, I sat on the stairs, you know, the stairs leading to the store. No matter creaky-old-Miss-Lonelyhearts-curmudgeon-forty-five-years-a-widow Vanessa—all sympathy aside, behavior's still behavior. Ten years I've had the studio, and she still calls me *Lorna.* She's completely befuddled by the cash register. Okay, let's give eccentricity a nod and a wink, and, let's face it, if she was suddenly *nice,* you'd drive her straight to the hospital. And as you like to say, it's all village life. But anyway, Simon, I heard what she said to you."

"And what I said back?"

"That, too. You were so upset, you tried, I think, to be chivalrous, but it came out—"

"Just pissed off, right?"

"Deeper, I'd say."

"I think you should just tell me, Lorca, what you want to tell me, okay?"

"I thought about that exchange all the rest of the day. And here's what: all along, you've known the line I'm so inspired by with my Emily Dickinson paintings is *We talked between the rooms,* right?"

"It's been interesting to me. You've never based your paintings on a poem before, not that I know of."

"These paintings being an exception may have some import here, I don't know, but when I heard Vanessa so crudely say, 'She's taking your wife away from you,' it struck a chord. Somehow and some way, it struck a chord. And I don't mean struck a chord just in me, but obviously in you as well, darling."

"Got my dander up, didn't she."

"It reminded me of that line from Gina Berriault you love so much."

"*The upsettedness is with me again.*"

"That's the one."

Lorca reached across the table and we did what we hadn't done in some time, which was to hold hands while talking. No matter how long you've been married, it makes a difference, that. "Vanessa saying what she said made me want to poison her tea," Lorca said. "And I still might. It's just that a deep chord gets struck, maybe because some truth's got revealed."

"That truth is?"

"I think for at least the last year—I haven't x-ed a date on the calendar or anything, but I think for at least the last year—which more or less coincides with when I've been working on this series—you've felt your wife *has* been taken away from you. Or that I've been somewhat absent, or not really locatable."

"You mean — I think you mean — we've been talking between rooms. But not really in rooms, together."

"That's maybe too literal a way to see that line, but yes, that's pretty much it," Lorca said.

"Talking between the rooms —"

"You and I always agreed that if we ever went into couples therapy again, in the first session we'd murder the therapist. It'd be homicide in Montpelier. And besides, every therapist we know in the area who conducts couples therapy has a shit marriage themselves."

"When we were trying to conceive a child — when we were trying to have a child, Lorca — it seemed couples therapy might help, didn't it?"

"It helped to talk about it, Simon. But it couldn't help the problem itself."

"Nor could all the medical examinations. Nor could all the tests. Nor could the fertility clinics, the injections, every sort of thing. We finally came to understand this, didn't we, as much as we possibly could."

"I'm not so desperate or daft, darling, to think that *between the rooms* — I mean, I'm not some goddamn Jungian mystical bullshit person, am I? — to think that *between the rooms* means forever stuck between not having a child and having a child. Or any such nonsense. I'm only saying that privately, up in my studio thinking thinking thinking, and maybe wanting us to talk to somebody about our difficulties — our being unlocatable to each other — I finally realized it would have to be us talking to each other. It has to be."

"And it's snowing out. We're having tea. Here we are."

"I will confess that for at least a year I've been in despair about us," Lorca said. "So—for me, we talked between the rooms—it's felt like we're living, breathing, talking, even making love—on too-rare occasions—everything between the rooms. Which may be like saying between real life and something else, but I can't for the life of me say what that something else is."

"That is the same as—but better put—what I've been feeling, too."

"Mutual sadness unspoken, maybe."

We talked for another three hours or so. More about our not being able to have a child—the old subject, but it somehow never seemed far away. Of disappointments. Of a fall from grace with my writing. Her doubts about her painting, though her work was selling well and her gallery was pleased. Adding to and subtracting from the ongoing and at times indulgent mentions of our ups and downs. But none of it felt un-useful—plus, there were no violins playing. No violins, only the exhausting bereavements, the sustaining gratefulness for marriage itself, all of it somewhat awkwardly put, which meant unrehearsed. Though we detoured and digressed, the conversation seemed to help organize our emotions, at least for the rest of the night. Of course, now I will never know if Lorca realized, during her saying all that she said, somewhat unprecedented in her forthrightness and the stalwart intensity of effort to hold back tears, that I loved her more deeply and fully than I ever had. And while it might be complete self-delusion, I felt that she was experiencing something of the same toward me. However, I didn't really know then, and can never know, if two people can love each other equally at any given moment, or that there is anything but intuition that can measure such a thing. What I do know is, that night was the last time we made love. Because the next morning I drove to Bar Harbor. I stayed at an inn overlooking the ocean. I got to the dock an hour early for the 7:00 a.m. ferry, scheduled to arrive in Yarmouth at 4:15 p.m. I was holding a copy of *In the Dutch Mountains,* looking at dolphins flying through the water alongside the ferry, when I keeled over at the rail. I keep thinking of the time I joked at a dinner with friends that I was envious of people who had repressed memories; at least I *thought* I was joking. Lorca had said, "Well, it might be enviable, but only if you get to choose which ones to repress." Anyway, things have changed, and now—today—I feel I want to remember everything. I don't mean this in a sentimental way, either. It is just that both the sadness and the happiness of everything that came before, especially in my marriage with Lorca, now feels equally part of this ongoingness.

NERVOUS COLLAPSE

MURIEL'S SEMESTER ended on December 10, 1994. She had a December 17 deadline to write a five-thousand-word critical review of a book called *The Poetry and Poetics of Nishiwaki Junzaburo: Modernism in Translation* by Hosea Hirata. She'd been working on it for months. I'd seen a few drafts on her desk in the library and even read a few pages. To my knowledge, Muriel didn't discuss her academic writing with Zachary except in a general way, though he frequently asked, "How's the writing coming along?" From what I could gather, the lengthier, more detailed conversations took place between Muriel and Kazumi Tanaka, in person and on the telephone. Muriel was now teaching an essay-writing workshop at the University of New Hampshire, a requirement for all freshmen, and a senior honors course of her own design.

On Tuesday nights during a semester, Muriel stayed at Kazumi's house. Muriel and Kazumi were considering co-translating a volume of autobiographical poems by Junzaburo, who had died in 1982, but Muriel's first priority was to expand her dissertation on Mukei Korin to meet the satisfaction of her editor at Oxford University Press, where she'd finally signed a contract in November. The fact that her teaching evaluations were top rated, along with news of the early acceptance of her dissertation as a book, would, she and Kazumi felt, give her a leg up on a tenure-track position opening at their university the following autumn. "But don't buy champagne quite yet," Muriel had said to Zachary. "It's a very competitive situation." It was my impression that while they both recognized that Zachary was certainly interested in Muriel's scholarship, he knew better how to be interested in her students and colleagues. He truly enjoyed hearing about all sorts of Machiavellian subterfuge in her department, gossip of every stripe, the numbing redundancies of faculty meetings, and whatever she could inquire, within received notions of propriety, during office hours with her students, and the information they volunteered that she wished she hadn't heard. "I'm not reckless in these conversations," she said, "but at the same time, I'm all ears."

That autumn semester, 1994, Muriel often spoke of a student in her honors course, Traditional Japanese Literary Forms—haiku, haibun, poetic diary, prose poem—whose name was Ardith Paleo. "Older than most graduate students, maybe thirty-three, divorced, no kids, drop-dead gorgeous, trust fund," Muriel said. "An IQ probably off the charts, if they still have IQ charts anymore, fluent in Mandarin and Japanese, already writes publishable stuff, and every class session she shows off a repertoire of imperious hurt and offended expressions. Haughtiness itself, and she's sort of cruel. Inventively so, but still."

"Well, you've noticed a lot," Zachary said.

"I guess I have, haven't I," Muriel said. "I suppose she has a talent for drawing notice."

"Maybe she thinks she's the professor. Or should be."

"On second thought, 'cruel' may not be exactly the right word. But let me tell you, last week she created a kind of private communication with me, right during class."

"What do you mean?"

"See, during our three-week concentration on haiku, I happened—and as you know, I seldom mention anything of my personal life in class—but I mentioned the haiku chiseled into Simon Inescort's gravestone, up by his writing cabin and the Japanese crabapple trees."

"Hey, even I can recite that haiku: *How far to | the end of the world? | Why, just a day's journey.* Basho, right?"

"You get an A, my darling. In class I said that in fact a haiku by Basho is written on the gravestone of the deceased husband of the woman we bought our farmhouse from. I said you may not have read any of Simon Inescort's novels, but that's what's written on his stone. And that's pretty much all I said."

"And this drop-dead-gorgeous, brilliant, haughty student responded in some—"

"*Provocative*—maybe not quite hostile, but definitely over-the-top way. That's how I experienced it at least. See, what finally happened was, I'd assigned each of the seven students a ten-page essay on a particular haiku. They had hundreds to choose from, all those anthologies and collections. A very wide range."

"And yet this Ardith Paleo chose the haiku on Simon Inescort's gravestone."

"What a fine detective you are."

"I can't find Corrine Moore, though."

Once Corrine became a presence, there had to be a hiatus in the conversation. It was late afternoon: dusk in the offing, clear sky, both bedroom and living room woodstoves at work. Muriel prepared them espressos and they sat at the kitchen table, waiting for the recognitions to settle, and then returned to the conversation. Four inches of snow blanketed the ground; a murder of crows, using their different voices, were on and around the two apple trees closest to the farmhouse.

Then Zachary said, "Sorry. Please tell me."

"Miss Paleo was the first to volunteer to read her few allotted paragraphs out loud," Muriel said. "Turned out, though, she ignored the fact that she was sharing the class with other people, and she read three times as much as she was supposed to. But the content of what she read was the thing. First, she took to task an interpretation of the haiku by the greatest Basho scholar ever, Makoto Ueda. And while she made a few good points, it was all too devoted to just being — oppositional. Sorry, I'm using academic-speak, aren't I?"

"Oh, I get 'oppositional' — arguing for the sake of arguing."

"Yeah, that's what it seemed with Miss Paleo. But then she more or less went after Simon Inescort, poor man."

"What's Simon have to do with the study of haiku?"

"That's what I mean by 'over the top.' She mocked the fact he had a haiku on his headstone. And then she formed a hypothesis having to do with it being a Western appropriation of Eastern thought, or something like that."

"But didn't everyone in the class see exactly what she was up to? Currying favor by being —"

"Oppositional? But I don't think she was currying favor, Zach. Whatever she was doing, the rest of the class was stunned."

"Did you ask Miss Paleo into your office for a good talking-to?"

"I think that's what she wanted. Personal time."

"So you left it alone?"

"No, I talked with Kazumi about it for hours and hours."

"But I'm hearing about it only now."

"I meant to tell you. But then there was this, that, and the other thing."

"What was Kazumi's take on it?"

"I think Kazumi was of two minds. First mind: it was hateful."

"And second?"

"I think she found Miss Paleo attractive."

BY DECEMBER 20, 1994, Zachary had followed up on eleven reported sightings of Corrine.

"Your nerves are shot," Muriel said. "If you don't ask Mr. Vlamick for a ten-day break, I'm going to call him up myself."

"How can I tell the Moores I'm going on vacation?"

"I'm marching right over to the phone, Zach."

They ended up going to Montreal for New Year's and then up to Quebec City for a week. During this time, I listened to all eleven reports on Zachary's tape recorder. I listened in the chronological order in which the individual follow-ups of purported sightings took place. In the sixth one, I could hear Zachary's exasperation so intensely ratcheted up, his voice broke a few times on the recording.

This is from the sixth recording:

"'Disappointments are often in direct relation to expectations, so don't raise your expectations too high,' Mr. Vlamick said to me about the Corrine Moore case. And yet, here I went and allowed that very thing to happen with a Mrs. Louise Kirchner, who lives in the village of Lincoln, not far from Vergennes. So goddamn stupid of me. I might be losing it. I feel like such an amateur.

"Okay — let me chronicle what happened. On the phone, Mrs. Kirchner sounded intelligent. 'I imagine you're getting a lot of crank calls in a horrid situation like that poor little girl's' — and see, right there, just her saying that, that should've been a red flag. On the other hand, I'm obligated to follow up, aren't I? The thing was, Mrs. Kirchner said she'd taken down a license number. I asked her to repeat the license number, and I jotted it down. Then I immediately called the DMV and asked them to call the state police with the owner's name, assuming Mrs. Kirchner got the plate number right. Then I drove over to interview Mrs. Kirchner.

"She lives in a beautiful Victorian-style house, oak-lined streets and all of that. She had coffee and raisin cookies all set out. Mrs. Kirchner herself was about seventy-five or so. We sat down and I said, 'To report seeing a missing child is taken with great seriousness, Mrs. Kirchner.' Small talk, and then I said, 'I understand that you yourself saw Corrine Moore.'

"Let me read from my notes: 'Yes, it was most definitely the child on the poster at our post office,' she said. 'I still have very good eyesight. You'll notice I don't require eyeglasses. Little Corrine was sitting in the front seat of a dark green Datsun pickup truck. You have the license number.'

"I asked if Corrine was sitting alone, and Mrs. Kirchner said yes. She supposedly saw Corrine in front of the Lincoln general store on East River Road. Mrs. Kirchner said she'd gone to the store at ten a.m. on November twenty-eighth to return two books to the bookmobile parked near the store. The bookmobile stops there three mornings a week. Mrs. Kirchner wrote down the titles of the two books she returned: *The Lottery Winner* by Mary Higgins Clark and *Girl Missing* — red flag, red flag, red flag — and the author of that book was Tess Gerritsen.

"'All right,' I said, 'thank you for that. *Girl Missing* is an interesting title, don't you think?' I said. To which Mrs. Kirchner replied, 'Oh, that book's about a serial killer in Boston. We don't have those in Vermont.' 'That's good to know,' I said.

"The interview lasted about an hour. I went through everything five, six, seven times. She was as calm as a nun — one of Muriel's pet phrases.

"So, it was all cordiality and certitude on Mrs. Kirchner's part. I thanked her profusely and left. Two hours later, I'm informed that the license plate indeed belongs to a 1990 Datsun pickup. The problem is, the truck is registered to a Mr. Walter Kirchner, age ninety-three, presently in the Vergennes Retirement Village, where he's been in residence for eight years.

"The next morning, I gave my preliminary report to Mr. Vlamick at the office and then drove back to Lincoln. I'd obtained the bookmobile schedule and waited in front of the general store, where it arrived at ten-twenty a.m. I interviewed the driver, whose name is William Iacone. Fellow about fifty years old, who also is part-time at the general store and does home deliveries of groceries in Lincoln and some neighboring towns. 'Oh, yes, Mrs. Kirchner,' Iacone said. 'She's got one bat left in her belfry and even that one isn't often home. She cleans up nicely, Mrs. Kirchner does. Mr. Kirchner left her in funds.'

"I asked the whereabouts of the pickup truck. 'Try her garage,' Iacone said. 'By the bye, Mrs. Kirchner blames her husband for just about every crime she reads about, especially in the *Crime Log* out of Barre. Also some of the bigger crimes in history.' I asked what he meant by the bigger crimes. 'Well, start with World War One,' he said.

"End of report on Mrs. Louise Kirchner of Lincoln, Vermont."

LORCA WAS INVITED for dinner at the farmhouse on January 23, 1995. It was a bitter-cold evening. I saw her headlights sweep the bare trees at around seven o'clock. Lorca was never, ever late for dinner; she appreciated the finer calibrations and timing of a host's cooking. In fact, Muriel had prepared chicken Marbella. Zachary was going to be late, as he was following another lead. When Lorca stepped into the house, I saw that she looked so lovely, and so tired. She wore blue jeans and a thick turtleneck sweater. "Sorry for my old-lady braids," she said. "I've been working day and night." It was the first time I had seen her in nearly two weeks, which is when she'd last sat in my cabin, sipping coffee from a take-out cup while talking to me—or thought she was—there in the one-gravestone cemetery near my cabin, within its ten-by-fifteen-foot stone wall.

Muriel had decided that the meal would be served in the living room rather than at the dining table, and it was all co-zily done. I did notice that once the food was served, Lorca didn't budge from her place on one of the sofas. I think she didn't want to look upstairs, or step into the library, or any-thing of that nature; my death was still too close.

After about an hour of quiet but good conversation, Zachary showed up. He filled a plate with chicken Marbella, then sat next to Muriel on the sofa. Lorca said, "Zachary, do you mind if we talk about Corrine Moore?" Zachary looked at Muriel, less, I think, for permission than to let her know he acknowledged—and wanted her to—that people were just going to ask. It was therefore tender and important that Muriel took Zachary's hand in hers and immediately framed things in the most personal of terms. "Zach's having a ner-vous collapse," she said. "I don't mean that the work's too much—no, he's very professional, very on top of things. Going about it methodically, and I'm more impressed by the hour. It's just—"

"Well, Zachary, a missing child—Corrine—and you're searching on Johanna and Devon's behalf, and of course

Corrine's," Lorca said with a certain formality of tone, which seemed mainly about treading lightly. "I don't mean just the fact that the family's hired you. Who else but God can they invest hope in, when you think about it. They aren't very religious, the Moores. As for the toll it's all taking on you — well, it's a *child,* for goodness' sake. Why on earth would you want to be a man who *wouldn't* have a nervous collapse? That depth of feeling doesn't have to contradict professionalism, now, does it?"

"Then there's the whole community, too," Muriel said.

"I've visited Johanna and Devon quite often lately," Lorca said, shifting into a more casual tone. "Downstairs in the co-op. People come in and sit by the stove. Of course, everyone's all worked up every minute. In Adamant — and not just Adamant — I mean, a *missing child.* It's like everyone's in a crazed state of worry. And, I might say, fear. Fear that Corrine is dead. Sorry to be so blunt."

"How is my husband thought of with all of this?" Muriel asked. "Because Calais is our home now."

"Highly thought of, Zachary, you're highly thought of. The fact that you called that initial meeting. The fact that you contact the Moores every single day. The fact that you keep everyone at the co-op so informed. Thoughtfulness counts for a lot. It's just regular people talking, what with ten thousand emotions an hour, about a child everyone's seen growing up. This may sound strange, but it's almost like, as long as people keep talking about Corrine — saying her name — she stays alive. Because people can lose heart. A whole community can lose heart."

"It's all been a strange way for me and Zach to discover

our new home," Muriel said. "The saddest of possible reasons helping us realize we chose the right place to raise a family."

"Are you working on that?" Lorca brought her hand to her mouth. "Oh, sorry, none of my business."

"That's okay, Lorca," Muriel said. "We'll talk."

"Yeah, it's been interesting," Zachary said, "who comes out of the woodwork in a case like this. I've met a few real loony tunes. Still, every Monday and Saturday, I go through every page of Corrine's file. What am I missing? What am I missing? I've had a few long talks with Erica Heilman, next door. I know she's considered *the* reputation, as far as detectives go."

"Erica's a straight shooter," Lorca said. "She knows life here very, very well. You can't go wrong listening to her."

"We're meeting again next week," Zachary said.

Lorca left the house around ten o'clock. While Zachary was clearing dishes, the telephone rang. Muriel picked up. "Oh, hey, Kazumi. Yep, I have time to talk. Our guest just left and Zach's on kitchen duty. Let me get the phone in the library, okay?"

Muriel held up the kitchen phone, and Zach took it from her. He held it until he heard that Muriel was on with Kazumi, then set it on its cradle. He loaded the dishes in the dishwasher and sponged the countertop. Of course, I could only hear one side of the phone conversation. It started out with academic matters. I heard the name Nishiwaki Junzaburo, and then talk about the work they were doing on a translation. I heard Zachary go upstairs. On the phone, Muriel and Kazumi had a spirited debate about a single line: *the screech of a plow scraping a meteorite.* Muriel said, "Kazumi, your certitude doesn't automatically mean that you're correct. You sometimes have a tin ear in English." It took Kazumi a moment to respond. Then Muriel said, "You just can't stand to be wrong."

Muriel listened a moment, then said, "'— the joining of two discordant qualities.' That's Coleridge, isn't it? Are you referring to the line of poetry we're discussing, or to our friendship?" Laughter.

I was suddenly aware of Zachary sitting on the stairs, listening in. Not for very long, just a few minutes. All of this brought back my own experience of feeling acutely interested in, but essentially left out of, intense conversations Lorca had with the painter Jake Berthot about painting and painters. They had been friends since before art school. On Jake's visits, they'd sit through entire nights, talking. Even when they basically agreed on this or that subject, the air bristled with what Balzac called "insatiable probity." There was no end to it. Each conversation implied an ongoingness. Coming to conclusions was entirely beside the point.

This is to say that in my marriage to Lorca, there were realms of knowledge and emotion I could only listen in on. I suppose that sounds obvious, and yet, thinking about it while sitting in the library's rocking chair as Muriel spoke with Kazumi, I felt an overwhelming sense of loss. Because to listen in was still intimate proximity. I also deeply missed our indoor cat, Boris, who now lived with Lorca above the co-op. Lorca would pick him up and say, "Whoa, such a big, handsome boy."

Into the telephone, Muriel was reading from an essay

by the poet Cid Corman I'd seen on her desk, which was about his own translation of Japanese poetry. She was obviously trying to substantiate a point about the practice itself: "'—largely adaptations, rather than stick to any apparent rigidity of structure.'"

Silence on Muriel's end. Then she said, "Oh, I see you find that lazy, and even transgressive."

In another moment, the phone call ended.

Epilogue sensed me getting up to leave the library. He arched up in place on the typewriter, then fairly leapt to the floor and raced toward wherever he sensed I was. His loud meowing had a somewhat crazy edge to it. Muriel said, "Eppy, if you're hungry, try to be more gentlemanly about it."

But Epilogue, as so often happened, spun in a circle, loosed a guttural hiss, and snapped the air, as if trying to catch a moth.

"Jesus, okay, okay," Muriel said, shaking her head back and forth. She reached down to pick up Epilogue, but he jumped at least two feet up to a bookshelf, flipped nearly all the way over in the air, then ran to his water dish, where he lapped water for a good long minute, as if trying to calm down. "Zach," Muriel called up the stairs, "can you look up cat psychiatrists in the phone book, please?"

Zachary called down, "I couldn't quite hear you. I'll be right there."

When he joined Muriel in the kitchen, she was opening a can of Fancy Feast. "Our cat is meshugga," she said. "Just now he flew around the library like a dervish, no reason whatsoever. And—"

The alarm went off. Zachary hurried over and pressed the OFF code. The telephone rang, and when Muriel answered, she said, "The fucking alarm went off again." She listened a moment, then said, "Oh, Kazumi, yeah, I'll call you right back." She hung up, and the telephone immediately rang again. Picking up, Muriel said, "There is no motion in the library. There is nobody *in* the goddamn library. I'm looking at the panel: it's MOTION IN LIBRARY. Is that what you got?" She listened, then said, "But, sir, we never, ever, ever have the alarm set when we're home. And we're home. And MOTION IN LIBRARY — as you know — just went off. This is the reverse of that previous time, when I'd set the alarm, and when we got home, it wasn't set. I think you have to send Eddie or somebody out again. I'm not happy." She slammed the phone onto its cradle.

"Take five deep breaths," Zachary said. "Then go call Kazumi."

When Muriel was back in the library and Zachary up in his office, I had a kind of rapprochement with Epilogue. Cats, of course, live in a sensory world we humans can scarcely imagine; the closest I've come to some understanding of this was in reading *I Am a Cat* by Natsume Soseki. Truth be told, Boris, a Russian blue, was really Lorca's cat — he was with her in the studio day and night; he would sleep on her side of the bed at her feet; he would paw at the volume knob of the radio if Lorca was listening to NPR and not seeing fit to rub him behind his ears at the same time. Boris is eleven now. Somewhere around his seventh or eighth year, he developed the habit of tearing up a Kleenex or a sheet of drawing paper, a little hissy fit that indicated his water bowl needed to be filled to the top, which was the only way he would drink from it; if it wasn't filled at least almost to the top, he sometimes would splash the water with his paw or even knock the bowl over. Colleen, our vet, said certain cats have extra-sensitive whiskers, and don't like it when they so much as touch the top of a bowl. My guess is that if anyone was to count the number of drawings Lorca made of Boris, it would certainly be in the hundreds. Whereas toward me, every day Boris had to work himself up to ambivalence; only rarely would he deign to sit on my lap while I was reading; every so often his majesty would set a half-eaten mouse at my feet.

Strangely enough, Epilogue and I were okay in each other's presence, barring my freaking him out at least once a day. It must be, to Epilogue, like experiencing the symptom without knowing the cause, or some such analogy. Here he can sense me but not see me. But as I mentioned, we have rapprochements. For instance, after Muriel got testy about Epilogue's behavior in the library, exacerbated by the sounding of the MOTION IN LIBRARY alarm, Epilogue, going on whatever aggregate vibes I give off that allow him to draw a bead, found me and sat next to me on one of the living room sofas. He had his steadily purring engine idling for the better part of half an hour. But then Muriel, off the phone now with Kazumi, called out, "Epilogue, big boy, come on in here so I can properly apologize. Epilogue! Eppy Eppy Eppy, come on." He went right into the library.

EDDIE, THE ALARM TECHNICIAN, came out the next morning after Zachary left for the Green Mountain Agency. Eddie accepted a cup of coffee, then said, "Mrs. Anders, maybe we should disconnect the sensor under the Turkish rug. But leave the motion detector in the library alone. We can experiment a little. Don't worry, my boss says today's service call is gratis. We really don't want to lose you as a client."

"Let me think about this a minute," Muriel said.

Eddie sipped some black coffee, then, looking pensive, almost embarrassed, said, "Mrs. Anders, I'm hesitant to say something here. I want to tell you something about your house. But it's maybe none of my fricken business, okay?"

"Tell me."

"Okay, here goes. My wife—Rebecca. My wife has worked at the Vermont Historical Society for over ten years now. She knows a lot about old houses, with old deeds, with old architecture. And a few nights ago we were playing chess—she taught me. And she said that since I had been telling her about your farmhouse, this beautiful old farmhouse, and the problem with the MOTION IN LIBRARY, she got interested in your house. But rest assured, believe me, my wife's the most trustworthy of persons. Nothing I tell her about work does she mention. Not ever. So there's no concern there."

"I believe you, Eddie," Muriel said. "But where's this going?"

Eddie reached into his work notebook and took out a piece of paper. He handed it to Muriel. Muriel looked at it and said, "I'm holding the original deed to our house, am I right?"

"A photostat."

"This is wonderful of you. Thank you."

"No, no, please, it wasn't me, it was Rebecca. She wanted you to look closely at the deed. Maybe use a magnifying glass. You'll see in fine print there's what's called a ghost clause."

"Actually, Lorca Pell—Mrs. Inescort—told us about this ghost clause."

"Then you already know, if you experience a 'malevolent presence' or something, you can legally get Mrs. Inescort to buy back the house."

"Don't jump to any conclusions, please."

"Look, I never did any work for the previous owners. I know Mr. Inescort passed on. From what I heard at the Adamant co-op when I was in there for coffee, Mrs. Inescort is a very nice lady. She's apparently an artist, but an upright citizen. I don't know if you are acquainted with Mrs. Inescort, but I think you should have every confidence that she'd take you at your word and see to returning the purchase price of this house. Not that I believe in ghosts or anything, let me add."

Eddie finished his coffee, put the mug in the kitchen sink, said, "Let my office know if you want to experiment as I suggested. Goodbye now." He drove off in his truck, and Muriel right away telephoned Zachary. When he picked up, Muriel said, "Darling, I've just now read word for word the ghost clause in the original deed to our house."

FORMS OF PRAYER
IN VERMONT

IN THE *TIMES ARGUS* newspaper that Muriel and Zachary had a subscription to, I read about the Corrine Moore prayer vigil on December 18, 1994, held at the public ice-skating and hockey rink on Barre Street in Montpelier. The Zamboni had been decorated with a sash containing a sequence of photographs of Corrine, so that when Everett Fitzmorris, the Zamboni operator, rolled the lumbering machine along in front of the stands, people could see them fairly close-up. Over five hundred people attended, including rabbis, pastors, priests, a Quaker group leader, a representative from the nondenominational church in Irasburg, and a Buddhist monk living in Middlebury, whose saffron robes were visible beneath his thick fleece coat and snow leggings. Each of them said a few words into the microphone set up by the food-warming pans and led the crowd in prayers.

The headline of the page 1 article was "Many Forms of Prayer in Vermont for Missing Girl." Each of the prayers were, in fact, quite different in nature, but most simply asked for Corrine's safe return, and each prayer was given its own column on page 4. According to the article, after the prayers were said, there was an ice-dancing demonstration, followed by a hockey game between members of the state legislature and people who worked at the National Life Insurance Company. The entire event was catered by the New England Culinary Institute. Lenny's, an all-purpose clothing store in Barre, supplied extra mittens and stocking caps. Student chefs in their white smocks and high-rise hats served at a long table. Space heaters were set here and there, and a fire marshal was on hand. Ann Cummings, Montpelier's mayor, was the hockey announcer—according to the article, she had "listened to some hockey games on the radio in order to practice"—and the game itself ended in a 0–0 tie and resulted in "two sprained ankles and a broken hockey stick." The event raised $4,500 for the Missing Children's Information Project, sponsored by the Friends meeting house.

When Muriel and Zachary returned from the prayer vigil, they threw off their winter bundling and sat in front of the woodstove in the living room, thawing out, sipping hot cocoa. "That was quite the scene," Muriel said.

"Johanna and Devon weren't there," Zachary said.

"I'm sure no one expected them."

"Conspicuous by their absence. Completely understandable."

"To be stared at like charity cases, huh?"

"I doubt that would've happened, but I'm sure they were worried it might."

"When will you see them next?" Muriel asked.

"Tomorrow."

"Any sense how they're holding up?"

"Stoically—at best."

They sipped their cocoa for a few moments and then Muriel said, "Maybe a little off the subject, Zach, but hearing all those prayers, I want to ask: Do you have any thoughts on how we should raise a child? Religion-wise, I mean. You being half Jewish, half not, and me being Episcopalian through and through, neither of us with any deep devotion to either. Modern souls that we are, we could choose a separate one altogether. I don't know. I've entertained Quaker now and then."

"The prayer vigil really got you thinking about this."

"I guess so. But anyway, I forgot to tell you, I've started my red letter days, so this month didn't work out as we'd hoped."

"Not for not trying."

I SPENT THE REST of the evening and night after the prayer vigil in my cabin. Funny thing, I didn't even know if I needed the propane stove blazing or not, but I had it blazing. It somehow helped. There I thought a lot about Muriel and Zachary being so in sync about their desire to have a child. It was sweet and compelling and, as far as I could tell, entirely without ambivalence—though of course I wasn't privy to every hour of pillow talk, nor to their privatemost thoughts on the subject, nor their apprehensions, if they had any. Their conversation was a bridge to my own memories, and, crossing it just then, I began to think about Lorca's and my makeshift wedding in Wales and the years of trying to conceive a child ourselves. The heartbreak of it, the self-consciousness, the relentless preoccupation, the exhaustive giving up and trying again, the outsized sense of unfairness, the doctors, the lab work, the therapists, the fertility clinics, the separate budgeting for any and all new procedures, a few of which placed us in the hands of charlatans — but the investment of hope often has little to do with rational thought — the self-incriminations elevated, in desperate moments, to an almost theological level of regard. ("Medically, it's not supposed to be a problem for either of us, so is it just karma? Probably mine.") Even the somehow not feeling "normal." It is astonishing what one goes through, and wants to go through, as long as the ends justify the means. And the truth of it was, I don't believe that Lorca and I ever completely gave up. But possibilities seemed to fail us. And this will sound odd, but when Zachary recorded in one of his investigative reports, "What am I missing? What am I missing?," I was reminded of a night after Lorca and I had received yet more disappointing news about conceiving, lying on the sofa, hearing Lorca puttering for distraction in the kitchen, and racking my brains, *What am I missing? What am I missing?*, as if merely thinking more inventively would lead to a solution. Things should be stated directly, don't you think? We had even spent $3,000, and driven ten times between Vermont and Montreal, for Indonesian massage therapy supposedly designed to counteract infertility. By that point, we had pretty much lost how to differentiate between that sort of thing and any conventional path. What we could not give up on was hopefulness.

Much earlier in our relationship — after two years of my waiting tables in Providence, two years of Lorca's teaching part-time at RISD, using our apartment's living room as a studio—my novel *The Plovers* was published. It was translated into French, Norwegian, and Dutch, and had a British edition, too. Despite all the insistences of ambition, the failed manuscripts, all of the fits and starts, this was beyond my wildest dreams. There was little fanfare, but reviews were for the most part very good; this brought in enough money so that I could severely budget in order to quit waiting tables, at least for a while, but certainly no riches. And there arrived an invitation to the literary festival in Hay-on-Wye, Wales, the "village of books."

It was during the festival that Lorca and I decided to get married. So we approached the director of the festival to get word out on our behalf that we needed a justice of the peace. The festival tradition was to pair an unseasoned writer with a seasoned one; I was paired with the famous Anthony Burgess. Lorca and I were staying at the Swan Hotel in the center of Hay-on-Wye. Bookstores were all up and down the main and side streets of the village. In fact, within an hour of getting off the train from London, we'd discovered C. Arden, a bookseller that specialized in natural history and travel, and had a glassed-in case full of rare first editions. I noticed a signed copy of *Journal of a Landscape Painter in Corsica* by Edward Lear. I very much wanted to take a look at this volume, but we were in a bit of a rush and had to get ready for my reading. Still, I thought, A copy signed by Edward Lear himself! On the small placard beside it: "Includes a self-portrait sketch." It was very expensive.

Lorca saw the book I was staring at through the glass. "It's perfectly okay by me, darling," she said. "I'm fine with no dinners out for ten years. Plus, I've always wanted to try painting with tubes of toothpaste. Paint is so pricey. Shall we sublet our room at the Swan? I'm fine with anything you're fine with."

"If it was a signed Old Testament, I could walk away," I said. "But it's a signed journal by Edward Lear."

"Tell me, love, who would even sign an Old Testament Bible?"

Already we were having a very nice time.

The entertainment for that year's festival was Van Morrison. "I'd leave you for him," Lorca said when we saw a poster for his performance, scheduled for the next night. "Even for a cup of coffee together. He'd have to call me honey-babe first. But not necessarily right away." In fact, we saw him sitting with friends in the pub of the Swan Hotel. He was wearing a Van Morrison T-shirt under his sports jacket, untucked over jeans, and he had on a pair of motorcycle boots.

My and Burgess's joint reading was at 7:30. When Colin Mac-Cabe, the master of ceremonies, stood at the microphone, he said, "We have had an unusual request. Our first reader tonight, the novelist Mr. Simon Inescort"—I was sitting on a chair just offstage—"we understand wishes to marry the painter Lorca Pell, here in Hay-on-Wye." He pointed to Lorca in the front row, and applause erupted and someone shouted "Well done!" "However," Colin continued, "they need to be married by a licensed clergy or justice of the peace or some such legal formality—I'm told an American would be best, Lord knows why. So if you know or are such an esteemed person and wish to marry this debut author and his beloved fiancée, do please see them after the reading."

Laughter and more applause. From the expression on Lorca's face, she could not have been more surprised. When she looked at me, I could only shrug. Then MacCabe gave his brief introduction. I was instructed to read for twenty minutes, max. I began by saying what an honor it was to be on the same stage as Anthony Burgess. From somewhere off-stage, Burgess, in a bellowing voice, said, "You pissing well should be, you fuckin' upstart!" Which brought a different tenor of laughter, also a spatter of applause. I could only manage to say, "I saw Mr. Burgess earlier in the pub. He's had a head start on me, I'm afraid. But imagine me thinking I could catch up with Anthony Burgess in any way."

Burgess read from his novel *Napoleon Symphony* and both the content and presentation were riveting. He received a standing ovation. When he got backstage, his assistant handed him a flask. He looked at me, raised the flask, took a deep swig, and said, "Best we not be formally introduced, don't you think? All right, then, lad, I'm off. Dinner plans and all that." I loved this encounter and described it a number of times over dinners in the farmhouse, one of my redundant anecdotes, always imperfectly recalled. Still, I did love that incident, back on the day Lorca and I got married.

We had dinner alone at the Swan, at a corner table. We could see the Burgess party at the opposite end of the large room. Lorca looked ravishing in black cotton pants, a white silk blouse, and a Japanese scarf with a pattern of white cranes. In London, she'd had her hair cut shorter than I had ever seen it. She wore a very pale red shade of lipstick. Once we'd discussed the menu, ordered, and clinked glasses of white wine, Lorca reached across the table, took my hands in hers, and said, "You were handsomely nervous, Simon. Oops, that didn't come out quite right. But nervous as you were, the part you read was well chosen. Perfect for the audience. Could you even tell the response was good?"

"Not really."

"Well, it was. It was good. I thought you might've been within your rights to read a few minutes longer. But better to err on the side of modesty, right? Also, your old sports jacket went well with the new shirt I got you in London."

"Thank you. I'm glad it's over."

"I've got to mention, though, my darling, for future reference maybe, since you'll be doing more readings. At public events, on the radio, et cetera. Please remember, you pronounce it *roar-shock*. You know, when you say your detective character has a *roar-shock* splotch of coffee on his shirt."

"Oh, shit, how did I pronounce it?"

"*Ror-sack,* or something like that. Maybe think of a lion's roar and an electric shock. Roar-shock. Why not write it on the back of your hand?"

"That's not a bad idea."

"Did I embarrass you just now, sweetheart?"

"No. Never."

"Look at it this way. We're here in Wales, so you suddenly decided to pronounce that one word with a thick Welsh accent."

We were sipping cognac after dinner, all romantically given to the evening, when a woman stepped up to our table. She was about forty, beautiful, with an open and welcoming countenance, and later Lorca told me she recognized her from the audience.

"Excuse me. I'm a licensed justice of the peace in Vermont," she said. She shook hands with Lorca and said, "My name's Sandra Robinson." Then Sandra and I shook hands, and I gestured for her to sit down with us. "I live in Calais, Vermont, about a twenty-minute drive from Montpelier, the state capital. It's C-a-l-a-i-s, probably everywhere else pronounced *Calay.*"

"We're pretty short on funds," Lorca said.

"You know something," Sandra said, "I couldn't care less about that. And I don't know if marrying you would even be legal here in Wales. No license and so on."

"We hadn't considered that part," I said.

"Here's my thought," Sandra said. "We have a witness — my husband, Peter, has already volunteered at my strong suggestion. As for getting a wedding photograph taken, Peter's a good photographer. He's got a camera. He's also volunteered for that purpose. Then, once you get back to the US, if in fact that's where you'll be living —"

"So far we live in Providence, Rhode Island," I said.

"Good. That's an easy drive to Vermont," Sandra said. "You contact me in advance. Drive up, I'll meet you in Montpelier, and we'll go to City Hall. I know everyone who works there. We'll iron it all out. If need be, we can have another ceremony, real quick vows. But anyway, I'll vouch for your marriage here in Wales. We'll write it up on Swan Hotel stationery, and sign and date it. Peter and I are staying there. Each room has five sheets of stationery. You're at the Swan, too, aren't you?"

"Yes," Lorca said. "This is all so great. What's your fee, though? I'm sorry, I want it on the up-and-up."

"Well, let's see now," Sandra said. "Simon — we enjoyed your reading, by the way. Do you think you might get Anthony Burgess over there to sign a copy of his book for me?"

"I don't really know him," I said.

"I bet he'd come around."

"Do you have the book with you?"

"Right here in my handbag."

Sandra took out her copy of *Napoleon Symphony* and handed it to me, then handed me a pen. I walked right over to Burgess's table. I stood behind him while he finished a story he was telling, which was being received with uproarious laughter. Burgess turned and noticed me standing there, but said nothing. When his story ended, I placed the book on the table in front of him and said, "Mr. Burgess, see that lady in the patchwork dress over there, looking so hopeful? She's an American justice of the peace and willing to marry me and my fiancée, Lorca. For her fee, all she wants is a signed copy of your book. She's already purchased it, as you can see." I set the pen down next to the book. He looked around the table at the expectant faces of his friends. "Well, now, son, that's quite the responsibility put on my wide shoulders, isn't it?" He signed the title page with great flourish, handed the book to me, stood up unsteadily, bowed, and received applause. He caught his balance, touched each of my shoulders with the pen, and said, "I hereby bestow my blessing on you and your bride." He got me into a kind of bear hug, lifted me up, and set me down. He waved me off like a servant. I loved this encounter, too, every moment of it.

I delivered the book to Sandra Robinson. "Fair exchange,

I think," I said. "He signed the book and kept your pen." This made Lorca laugh, which often was all I most cared about.

"Want to get married now?" Lorca asked.

"Let me get Peter," Sandra said.

In five or so minutes, she returned with her husband. He shook Lorca's hand, then mine, and said, "Peter Wells." He held up his Nikon camera, which was slung around his neck on a braided cord. "Wedding photographer for hire." Peter was a strongly built man with a rough-hewn, handsome face that, in my opinion, should be on the hundred-dollar bill — it was that commanding.

"My husband's a blacksmith associated with the Lake Champlain Maritime Museum," Sandra said. "Me, I direct the Office of Adult Literacy, right in Montpelier."

Sandra held out the Bible she'd taken from her room. "I've got the goods right here. No matter what your religious affiliation, or none at all, it's the necessary prop."

"I have no idea where to get married around here," Lorca said. "But Simon, remember the C. Arden shop? It had a nice courtyard garden out back."

"We could ask," I said.

The four of us marched the two blocks to C. Arden, whose hours, according to the sign, were 10 a.m. to 11:30 p.m. "Imagine that, a bookstore that's open to nearly midnight," Sandra said. "This is my kind of place."

We trundled in, and the proprietor walked up and said, "Mrs. Everson. Owner of the shop. Any subject in particular you're interested in?"

"Marriage," Peter said.

"We've got nothing in stock. Sorry."

"Mrs. Everson," Lorca said. She took me by the arm and pulled me forward. "I'm Lorca Pell. Simon Inescort, here, and I would like to get married in your courtyard."

Mrs. Everson was about eighty and no-nonsense. "Want to browse before or after? You'd only have half an hour or so before closing."

"I think after," Lorca said.

"Step right outside, then," Mrs. Everson said. "Might you need a witness?"

"We could use a third one," Lorca said.

"Just a moment," Mrs. Everson said. She walked to the front door, flipped the OPEN sign to CLOSED, then followed us into the courtyard. "I'll open again once your nuptials are completed."

Out back, there was a stone wall and garden, two bird feeders on poles, a marble-top table with two chairs, a small birch tree near the stone wall.

"We don't have rings," Lorca said.

"Take mine," Mrs. Everson said. "I'm not daft, it's just for the moment. My husband's long dead, but he wouldn't disapprove anyway."

Mrs. Everson slid off her ring and handed it to me. Caught up in the spirit of things, Peter slid off his wedding band and handed it to Lorca. Sandra broke into such intense laughter, tears rolled down her face. She kissed her husband right on the mouth.

That is how it proceeded, our wedding. Not thought out or hesitated over. Instead, all practical urgency, five people, most complete strangers to each other, only one a resident of a town of books, all collaborating on Lorca's and my whims, outside of the expected way an evening might otherwise have unfolded. And now we were all permanently connected by what the writer Jean Rhys might've called a marriage incident.

After the "I do" part, Sandra came up with an off-the-cuff little speech that included, "A long marriage is a lot like something else, but I can't think what just now." This was our wedding party. This was our entourage. These were our witnesses. Lorca and I were pronounced man and wife; we had a long, excellent kiss in the courtyard, with its two old-fashioned gaslights and night birdsong. We gave back the rings, and Mrs. Everson brought out a bottle of whiskey from her storeroom. "I've only got teacups," she said.

We raised a toast to all of us together, a second was offered by Peter to Lorca's and my marriage, and then Sandra said, "Ah, a wedding night at the Swan Hotel. Peter, let's have one of those, too."

Peter snapped an entire roll of film. "Leave your address at the counter. I'll send these to you," he said. "Congratulations." He and Sandra walked off hand in hand toward the hotel.

Mrs. Everson turned the sign back to OPEN. Lorca and I stood near the cash register. We didn't quite know what to do or say, perhaps even how to feel properly exhilarated. "Half price off any book for the newlyweds," Mrs. Everson said. "It's a one-time-only policy I've just decided on."

I think we were relieved to have the distraction. "There was a book of Caravaggio's I saw," Lorca said.

"My first wedding gift to you," I said.

Lorca went over to the art section. I headed toward the glass case. Mrs. Everson walked over to Lorca, tapped her on the shoulder, pointed to me, and said, "Shall I give your husband the key? It's all expensive first editions in there."

"Yes, give him the key, Mrs. Everson," Lorca said. "But you might have to let me work off the cost in your bookshop. We'll have to sleep in the storage room, too, if you don't mind, because my husband's publisher only paid for one night at the Swan Hotel."

"In London I lived through the Blitz, so I've suffered worse," she said.

Mrs. Everson walked over to a table with an electric plate and kettle, boxes of tea, a sugar bowl, spoons, and cups. "Tea?" she asked.

"Yes, please," Lorca said. "Not for Simon, though."

"Right," Mrs. Everson said.

Soon she and Lorca were having tea together, sitting on a sagging sofa off near the natural history shelves.

"Look at me," Mrs. Everson said. "Mallalorking with newlyweds."

"I don't know that word," Lorca said.

"Mallalorking? Oh, it means 'restlessness before a journey.'"

"Are you taking a journey soon?"

"Just upstairs to bed, once the shop's closed up."

"I see."

"But at my age, up the stairs feels like travel."

In fact, I ended up purchasing the signed Edward Lear volume, and paid for it with a check, all the while knowing this transaction would all but spend down to nothing my first—and what turned out to be my only—royalty check. Walking back to the hotel, I mentioned this to Lorca. "Well, we bought each other wedding presents, didn't we," she said.

BACK IN THE STATES a month later, Lorca had an exhibition of her work in Boston. She sold four paintings; the proceeds allowed us to purchase the yellow Ford pickup. Leaving Boston on a very warm summer's day, we drove to Montpelier. We'd contacted Sandra ahead of time. Sure enough, she met us in town, at a restaurant called Horn of the Moon. Naturally, we took Sandra out to lunch: bread, soup, and a piece of cheesecake for dessert. Plus coffee. "I did some research on legal this and legal that," she said. "And you've got an appointment at three o'clock. City Hall."

"Already our second marriage," Lorca said.

"But the first in this country," I said.

"Come on, you two," Sandra said. "Cheer up. By three-thirty you'll be officially married in Vermont. It doesn't get better."

And so, with Sandra as our witness, we got married at City Hall in Montpelier. "Stay in touch," Sandra said when we parted. "After all, I'm the only one, other than yourselves, who's been at both your weddings."

"Please tell Peter thanks for the great photographs from our first one," Lorca said.

Before we checked into one of the old inns in Montpelier for the night, we decided to take a leisurely drive out to the countryside. We bought a gazetteer in a pharmacy, browsed awhile at Bear Pond Books, then drove up to College Hall, overlooking the town. We gazed back at the gold dome of the capitol, then headed north, turning off soon to the east, where we took a dirt road through rolling farmland and ended up in the village of Adamant, where we stopped at the co-op. "The guidebook says this is one of the oldest co-operatives in the state," Lorca said.

The front screen door to the co-op opened and a gray Scottish terrier wearing a kerchief around its neck came out, barked a few times at us, and trotted off up the road, where it chased a few Canada geese into a stone-rimmed pond, then continued on up the road. "That dog's really his own dog," Lorca said.

We stepped inside the co-op. The ambience felt out of the late nineteenth century, but with a telephone. The cash register was of such size and complexity, it looked like it might double as a calliope. There was a section displaying the work of local artisans: vases, handmade postcards, photographs of wildlife, knitted socks. The shelves were well stocked, as was the freezer. The maple syrup shelf was varietal. Crouched on high shelves were many different kinds of papier-mâché cats. Lorca immediately wanted to purchase a calico with a Cheshire grin and prominent whiskers. It went for $10. "Flatlanders usually get maple syrup, too," the woman behind the counter said. She looked to be in her late sixties, perhaps older, and was dressed in a loose-fitting sweater, dark slacks, and low-cut tennis shoes.

"What's a flatlander?" Lorca asked, slightly on the defensive; the tone taken by the clerk had warranted it, though.

"Not from Vermont," the woman said.

"I see," Lorca said. "Well, on second thought, I'll put this excellently made cat back on the shelf."

"Suit yourself," the clerk said.

"No, what suited me was the cat. What didn't suit me was what you called me."

"I always save my apologies for much later."

"How do you know I'm not from Vermont?"

"I'm a student of people."

Lorca reached into her book bag, which she'd purchased at Bear Pond Books. She took out our marriage certificate. She held it between her hands and displayed it up close to the clerk. "We just got married. City Hall. Montpelier."

"Jesum crow," the clerk said.

"What's that mean, some sort of reference to Jesus?" Lorca asked.

"Can I help you find anything else, young lady?"

"Yes, you can tell me who makes the papier-mâché cats, please. I'd like to contact the artist directly."

"Her name's Janet. Her studio's right upstairs. She doesn't like to be disturbed, though. She asked me to say that."

"Well, I'm afraid I'm going upstairs to tell Janet why she lost a sale. I'm going to say I set her calico cat on the cash register, but then it didn't work out. I'm going to tell her why."

"Do as you please."

"And I'm going to mention that—what's your name, may I ask?"

"Vanessa."

"That Vanessa isn't acting on behalf of her papier-mâché cats."

"I must've struck a nerve," Vanessa said. "Maybe you're upset about just getting married."

This was such a sharply cantankerous retort that I could see it took Lorca every ounce of strength for her not to smile and laugh. "Quite the opposite, Vanessa," Lorca said. "I've never been happier. In fact, today was the second time I married the same man. Simon Inescort, over there by the scones. I'm Lorca Pell."

"Well, do you live in Vermont or not?"

Then Lorca said something that surprised me. "No, but we're looking for a house here."

Lorca retrieved the calico cat and paid for it. Progress was being made left and right. "If you don't need an apology, and you don't tattle on me to Janet—she and I often have words—then I'll tell you inside information on a great old farmhouse fifteen, twenty minutes from here, in East Calais. On a road called Peck Hill Road. The present owner's a New Yorker. He finds it too quiet. He's assigned me to put the word out. No realtor involved. The house's got good luck for children, too."

"How do you mean?" Lorca said.

"Drive over and peek into the window. Right into the library. That library used to be the birthing room. There's still a gigantic woodstove in there. The Peck family built it somewhere mid–eighteen hundreds. There were three daughters. Each of the daughters was born right in the library. There's a big maple tree named after each daughter right out front of the house, too."

"Let's go look, Simon."

"Fine with me," I said.

I didn't know if it was fine with me or not. Suddenly there seemed to be something occurring, and it required an alertness to possibility.

"Can you draw us a map?" Lorca asked.

"Take the cat out of the paper bag," Vanessa said. "I'll draw a map on the side. No reason to waste a piece of paper."

She drew a map to Peck Hill Road.

In the car, Lorca said, "You know how everybody's trying to find out their ancestry? Like that ad we saw on TV the other night?"

"I remember that," I said.

"Well, I was thinking of finding out my ancestry as far back as possible. But now I'm not going to, because what if I'm related to Vanessa? I'd have to walk across the road there, to Sodom Pond, and drown myself."

"And yet you clearly — am I wrong? — already, sight unseen, love the house you wouldn't have even known about if it wasn't for Vanessa."

LORCA HELD THE BAG with the cat inside and called out directions. We drove down Adamant Road to Pekin Brook Road. We turned right on Pekin Brook until we got to Peck Hill Road, where we took a left. This took us past an old schoolhouse, then up a steep incline through thick woods.

"Vanessa's sent us the back way," I said.

"I'd prefer to think it's the not-known-to-flatlanders route," Lorca said.

Fifty or so more yards, at the rise, we first saw the house. "Look, there's the maples," Lorca said. They were indeed majestic shade trees, set between the dirt road and the house.

In another minute, we parked across the road. Lorca set the bag on the front seat and, standing on either side of the pickup, we looked at the house. It was white and needed paint. The roof was shingled; there were two chimneys. The front and mudroom doors were painted forest green. We walked up to look into the window at the far left. "It's the library," Lorca said. "There's the woodstove—Vanessa was right, and it's enormous."

We looked in through the living room window. "Look at the overhead beam," I said. "This big room used to be two rooms." We could see into the kitchen, all the way to the wide kitchen window at the back, and through it to what looked like a close wall of trees. But that was just skewed perspective—those trees had to be a few miles away. "The owner's got very nice taste," Lorca said. "The antique furniture. The lamps. And that big kitchen table. I'm dying to see the upstairs, though."

"It's getting a little dark, Lorca," I said. "Let's take a quick walk up the road, then maybe come back tomorrow."

"I have a stronger feeling than that."

"How do you mean?"

"I want to spend our second honeymoon night in this

house, Simon. I've just had that thought. And now it's already way more than a thought."

"What is it, then?"

"I don't know if I should say."

"Lorca, just tell me. Your face is all flushed. Tell me."

Lorca walked up and embraced me tightly. I could feel her taking deep breaths. She put her mouth to my ear and said, "I already see us living in this house, Simon. I *see* it."

I held her at arm's length. "Okay, let's drive back to the co-op. We'll find out the owner's phone number. Vanessa has to have it, right? Then we'll ask to call him, right then and there."

"And he answers the phone, then what?"

"Then we talk to him."

"No, we say, 'We want to buy your house. We love it and want to buy it. But we have to spend the night in it first, and may we please do that?'"

"Total strangers."

"We'll somehow get Vanessa to vouch for us."

"She won't."

"I'll buy the rest of the papier-mâché cats."

"Oh, that'll do it."

"You give up, then you don't," Lorca said. "It usually goes in that order. So, now, do we agree on the strategy?"

We drove back to the co-op. When we stepped inside, Vanessa said, "Forgot the maple syrup, right? Just joking."

Lorca walked to the counter. "Vanessa, it was so — *generous.* So generous of you to tell us about the house."

"The owner's name is Greg."

"We fell in love with the house, Vanessa."

"Did you think I'd think you wouldn't?"

"Well, you were right, then. You wouldn't happen to have Greg's telephone number by any chance?"

"Not by chance. But because Greg left it with me. Because why else would he make it my responsibility to get the word out, no realtor. I'm his official agent in this. He's a New Yorker; he liked my chutzpah."

"We'd like to call him right away," I said.

"Ten-dollar deposit," Vanessa said.

"For long distance?" I said.

"That's the ticket."

I handed her a ten-dollar bill. She rummaged around a bit, then found a slip of paper with the phone number on it. She handed it to me. "I'm listening in," she said. "This is a once-in-a-lifetime thing for me. I'll never be a real estate broker again. Use the phone right there."

I dialed the number. But Lorca took the phone from me. Vanessa said, "She wears the pants in the family, I see."

When someone picked up, Lorca said, "Is this Greg?" She listened a moment, then said, "I'm so happy you were home, Greg. My name is Lorca Pell. I'm standing with your trusted friend Vanessa, in the Adamant co-op. My husband, Simon, is here with me, too. We just got married at City Hall in Montpelier. Vanessa gave us a map to your house, and we went and looked, and it's absolutely the perfect house for us. Please please please tell us it's still for sale." Lorca crossed her fingers, listened, then said, "That is wonderful news. But we have a favor to ask. We'd like to spend tonight in the house.

I'm a painter, my husband's a novelist. His first novel was just published; we were over in Europe with it."

Lorca handed the phone to Vanessa. "Vanessa here," she said. "Look, Greg, to use your language, these kids aren't meshugga."

They talked a few more minutes, then Vanessa hung up the phone. She said, "Give me a sec." She dialed a number. "Hello, Erica? Vanessa Sprague at the co-op." Pause. "I'm fine, honey, but listen up. Your soon-to-be ex-neighbor, Greg, as you know, made me the local switchboard as far as selling his house is concerned. There's a young couple— write down their names? Lorca and Simon." Pause. "I don't know what you mean, 'like the poet Lorca.' Anyway, listen. They're coming over to spend the night in the house. Because they might buy it. I told Greg I'd call you at his request. He wants you to be aware of their presence." Pause. "Okay, honey, thank you."

Vanessa said, "I've just called your maybe future next-door neighbor, Erica. Last name of Heilman. She's a young private investigator. Has her own agency, consisting of herself. She hires out all over the state. She's been mentioned in the *Times Argus,* oh, maybe eight times. I think of her as the female Sherlock Holmes, minus we're not in London. Private investigator . . . *professionally.* Licensed to carry a firearm."

"You can't be too careful these days, huh, Vanessa?" Lorca said.

"Not since Adam and Eve, not since Cain and Abel, and all the rest of that crowd, you can't be too careful."

"Should we go over and introduce ourselves to Erica?" I asked.

"In my opinion, it's enough she knows you're there. But do what you think best. She'll see lights on."

Vanessa handed us the house key. "It's for the mudroom door," she said.

THE LONG AND THE SHORT of it was, we spent the night in the house. We only brought in our bathroom kits. Nothing else. We toured the house; the upstairs had a master bedroom whose view seemed to take in the world. It also had five doors, including closets and a bathroom. There were two other bedrooms and a guest bathroom off the hall. The east-facing bedroom had a view of the enormous three-story barn.

We fell onto the four-poster bed in the master bedroom. We lay kissing, and soon had our shirts off, and then Lorca said, "I want to do this in the library."

"The library—"

"On the red sofa in there."

When I woke the next morning, covered by a quilt, Lorca had already brought in two cups of coffee. She'd placed a book on top of mine to keep it warm. She wore only her long cotton frock. She must've walked out to the car, because the papier-mâché cat was on the library table. Without letting her know I was awake, I watched her sketch in her notebook. She kept looking over to the rust-red and brown stove with its intricate ironwork, so I figured that was her subject. When I said, "Good morning, sight for sore eyes," she said, "Sorry, darling, I've been up for hours. I saw the sun come up."

"You and this library look a natural fit."

"I'd want to keep it a library," she said. "I really hope we can get the house. Oddly enough, this morning it doesn't seem impetuous anymore." She handed me my cup of coffee. "You'd never say this, but I will: it's meant to be."

I sipped some coffee and said, "I think we should stay in town tonight. We can look around. Go to a restaurant, or a movie."

"That sounds right."

It was a blessedly quiet morning, is what I felt. There was some birdsong. It had lightly rained during the night, and now there was rain in the trees. Lorca had lifted a screen window, and we could hear it. That was, I remember, the first experienced paradox: no rain on the roof but rain in the trees, and over the years, I loved that each time it happened. "About an hour ago, I had my thinking cap on," Lorca said. "What occurred to me was the proximity of this big stove, and just ten yards or so away, the maple trees. Named for each of the Peck girls, born right in this room. The daughters are gone, but the trees aren't. I don't know what to call it, really. It's a kind of . . . ongoingness."

"Born in this room — amazing," I said. "It meant each of the daughters didn't have to begin their lives with a journey home."

Lorca continued to sketch. I finished the coffee and didn't want to move an inch.

Later in the morning, we walked over to our pickup. "I wonder if Erica Heilman next door dusted it for fingerprints," Lorca said. Using Vanessa's map, we backtracked to Adamant, where we left the house key at the co-op. At the inn, we apologized to the proprietor, Mr. Avasti, for not showing up the previous night. "We stayed in the house we're hoping to purchase, in East Calais," Lorca said.

"Welcome to Vermont, then," he said.

"We're staying on a few days," I said. "Do you have a vacancy?"

"Yes, same room, twelve, upstairs, here in the main building. Staying a few days? I won't charge you for the no-show."

Once in our room, Lorca asked if I'd call Greg in New York. She sat on the bed next to me as I dialed the number. When Greg answered, I said, "This is Simon Inescort. We spent the night in your house. Thank you. We love it there and we're hoping you'll sell it to us. We're very much hoping that."

"Vanessa said you passed muster," Greg said. "That is difficult to do with her. Now let's see what the bank says. If it works out, you can keep the washer and dryer. But I won't repair the mudroom. Of course, all of the furniture I'll put in storage. But I couldn't get to that for at least a few months."

"All fair enough," I said.

"You didn't find it too quiet?"

"We heard a few woodpeckers, someone's dog barking in the distance for a few minutes. There was a windy rain last night, too. Rain in the trees this morning. Not to mention our own voices."

"I get it. I understand. Fine. You'll have a good life there. I hope it all works out with the bank."

"I'm sure it will."

"Let's wait and see," he said. "Good luck."

"I should mention, we made coffee. But we cleaned up after."

IN VERMONT AT THAT TIME, if your credit was solid, you only needed to put down 5 percent of the purchase price of a house to get approved for a mortgage. Lorca wrote out a check for $12,000, from her inheritance. I contributed $2,500 from my writing. That left us $1,200 in our savings account and $200 in checking. Plus, I was due an $8,000 advance for a new novel.

We waited things out in Montpelier for three days. Finally the bank informed Greg that we were in good stead. An attorney he'd worked with wrote up a bill of sale and, in his office on Main Street, said, "Greg's going to be in Europe for a month. You've got his okay to start living in the house whenever you want." Before we returned to Providence, we drove to JCPenney at the mall and bought new sheets, pillowcases, towels. After checking out of the inn, we walked across Main Street and purchased a pair of iron candle holders in an antique store.

"All within a week," Lorca said as we pulled onto Route 89 south. "A marriage certificate and a bill of sale. Life seems to have started in earnest, don't you think?"

"Stop for coffee in Hanover, maybe?"

"That'd be nice."

We listened to the radio awhile. "If we conceived a child last night," Lorca said, "we definitely should plant a maple tree."

SCARECROW INVITES
CROWS FOR TEA

THE FIRST TIME Zachary spent the night at Johanna and Devon Moore's house was February 15, 1995.

The day before, Valentine's Day, Muriel and Zachary had planned to have dinner at home, just the two of them. Because she thought it might serve as a useful distraction, help counter the frustrations, insomnia, lags, and disappointments in the Corrine Moore investigation, Muriel had signed him up for the Soups and Stews course at the New England Culinary Institute, which met on three consecutive Thursdays, 6:30 to 9:00 p.m. Muriel felt he should take the class alone, but said, "I'll try everything you make, with gratitude and no judgment, unless it's awful." Zachary had attended only the first class so far, on *soupe au pistou*, a Provençal vegetable soup with pesto, and had intended to prepare the recipe for Valentine's Day dinner. He also purchased a heart-shaped chocolate cake and had the pastry chef write, in looping cursive, *Love of my life* across the top. He didn't care in the least how sappy this was. He placed a single candle in the middle. He'd spent the day in the office with Erica

Heilman. Mr. Vlamick had asked her to come out of detective semiretirement to help with the Corrine Moore case.

Zachary related to Muriel that Mr. Vlamick had said, "Erica's *the* reputation in this part of Vermont."

Erica had already been to the farmhouse once for dinner. She was forty-three, intense, dark-haired, lovely in an unselfconscious way, a touch raunchy in her speech, had read lots of novels. She'd worked on cases for the Green Mountain Agency a number of times. She was raising a son, Henry, alone. She wrote and appeared on a radio program called *Rumblestrip,* in-depth and unique, having to do with the more abject sociologies in Vermont, and was especially admired for her unpatronizing, fearless interviews. She had once dropped in on Muriel, who afterward told Zachary, "She's sick of dating plumbers and carpenters. On the other hand, they make house calls. I'm just quoting."

"I've studied up," Zachary said. "Our esteemed neighbor once was previously involved with a missing child case. Little boy named Brian Carasol, who went missing in Barre. *Poof.* Just disappeared one day. Erica worked on that day and night for six weeks. Mr. Vlamick handed me the pertinent file. I pored over it. The missing kid turned up in Maine, sitting in a bus station. There's not much similarity between that case and Corrine's, except of course the 'missing' part. But Erica's notes are almost an epic novel. She's really the cat's pajamas."

"You haven't seen her pajamas, have you?"

"Muriel, am I a plumber or carpenter?"

"You can't nail a picture on the wall. You can't change a spigot filter. You can type pretty well, though. But I guess that doesn't count. Kidding aside? In our woman-to-woman talk, Erica said she wants a serious relationship in her life. You aren't to know any of this."

"That's like in *Perry Mason,* where Perry delivers the coup de grâce but the judge says, 'Objection sustained. I must ask the jury to strike that from their consideration.'"

"What'd you feel when Mr. Vlamick said what he said?"

"I need help, Muriel. He knows I need help. He figured out Erica was the help I needed."

Back to Valentine's Day. Muriel usually got home from teaching somewhere near 7:30, and close to that time, the headlights of one car appeared, and within thirty seconds, the headlights of a second car. Car doors slammed and voices approaching the house could be heard.

It would've been hard not to notice Zachary's look of bewildered surprise when Muriel stepped through the mudroom door into the kitchen, followed by Kazumi Tanaka, followed by a third woman. Muriel looked into the living room, where Zachary had set a small table for two.

Muriel handed Zachary a small gift box with a ribbon. Without removing her coat, she kissed him deeply. "Swoon," she said. "Happy Valentine's Day, my love. The table looks so great. I'll just add two more place settings."

"Oh, me and Ardith can drive into Montpelier for our own Valentine's dinner," Kazumi said, giving Zachary a peck on the cheek. "That's no problem. Lovely to see you, Zach. What's on the stove?"

"*Soupe au pistou,*" Zachary said, speaking like Inspector Clouseau in *The Pink Panther.*

Ardith walked over to the stove, lifted the cover off the

pot, picked a wooden spoon from the jar of wooden utensils, took up a small portion of the soup, and tasted it. "Very, very good," she said. "Maybe needs salt."

"Zachary, this is Ardith Paleo," Muriel said.

Ardith reached out and shook hands with Zachary, placed the spoon on a strip of paper towel on the counter.

"Where'd you study French cooking?" Ardith asked.

"New England Culinary Institute," Zachary said.

Muriel looked at him with a curious expression, perhaps something like, *Come on, she's showing interest, in her own way. She's a guest. Lighten up.*

"Ardith's the student I told you so much about," Muriel said. "She graduated this past December. Midyear graduation."

"Nice to meet you," Zachary said. "But no, of course, seeing as Muriel's invited you, welcome. Let's all celebrate together."

"Make yourself at home, ladies," Muriel said. "Kaz, you know where the guest room is. Why not take Ardith upstairs and get settled."

Kazumi and Ardith went upstairs. They each had an overnight bag. Muriel gave Zachary another kiss and held it for a long moment. "It was all last minute, Zach. I love that you had everything waiting like this. I love it. It was all very sudden. It's rather brave of Kazumi, her being so private a person. Is that chocolate cake I see?"

"I didn't make it."

"That candle is the perfect touch."

Muriel took off her coat and draped it over a kitchen chair. She walked in and inspected the cake. Reading the words on it, she said, "Ditto for me, sweetheart. Love of my life, too. Are you upset?"

"Surprised, I guess."

"Just to make a fine point, Miss Paleo's graduated. They're both adults. It's two adults. And Ardith was never Kazumi's student."

"What am I, the university ethics police? Love is hard to find, for everyone, no exceptions, is what you always say. I agree. You were right, I must say. She's drop-dead gorgeous. Let me get out two more plates."

Muriel tasted the soup. "She's right, I'm afraid. It needs salt. Shall I do the honors?"

"Go ahead."

Muriel sprinkled salt in with the wooden spoon, stirred the soup, took another taste, and said, "That should do it. It's really delicious, Zach. Any French blood in your ancestry?"

"There was a great-uncle, my dad's side, who visited Paris once. My mother referred to him as a 'bounder.'"

"I think I taste everything your uncle learned in Paris."

"Thank you, Murr. But you know as well as anyone, this is a simpleton's recipe."

"I heard the instructor at the Culinary Institute's bombastic."

"He shouts a lot. But it's mostly in French, so it sounds important."

"Anyway, I'm sorry."

"Come on, Muriel. I just had another kind of dinner in mind. I'm fine with it."

"I'm sorry, sweetheart. Looking at the romantic tableau,

you can't be entirely fine with it. But we don't put guests out on the street, do we?"

"I picked up two excellent bottles of red."

"I've had dinner twice with them at a restaurant. Two bottles might not be enough."

"They're Château Haut-Brion. Didn't at all fall within our budget."

"You're getting fluent in French after one cooking class. I'm impressed."

"Those two like to drink, huh?"

"Being the detective, are we?"

"You want me to run a bath for you?"

"When's dinner?"

"I'd say forty minutes."

"Then yes to a bath."

Zachary went to the downstairs bathroom and ran the bath, sifting in lemon verbena bath salts. Back in the kitchen, he said, "Okay with you I don't put your Chopin on?"

"Yes, that's just for us. Not for company."

Muriel went into the bathroom and shut the door halfway. Zachary opened her gift: a paperweight that emulated a Victorian pocket watch, though much heavier, with a compass set into it. The Valentine card read: *To keep your papers in place. The roman numeral clock is to tell you when your evening's work is done — the compass is to give directions to our bed. Love from me and Epilogue, Murr.* "It's a very fine paperweight," he called into the bathroom. Thank you."

"You can use the compass later tonight," she said. He glimpsed her sink down into the bath. She said, "Mm-

mmm." I followed Zachary as he took the paperweight upstairs and set it on his desk. Then he sat down to read over
his day's notes from the investigation — he couldn't help
himself, apparently.

WHEN ANY GUEST FIRST ARRIVED, Epilogue flew into the big
closet in the master bedroom. He'd stay in there until he
sensed it was safe downstairs, and then he'd show up like an
opera singer making a grand entrance from offstage, dramatically meowing, with a leap onto someone's lap. He seemed
fairly indiscriminate about whose lap, or so it seemed. He may
have had his reasons. Yet with Kazumi and Ardith, something
unprecedented happened. Epilogue ran upstairs with them
to sit on the star quilt in the middle of their bed and wouldn't
budge. He all but demanded, with an insistent repertoire of
purrs and crescendos of yowls, and by rolling on his back, that
they rub his belly and scratch behind his ears. He loudly protested when they left the room to go downstairs for dinner.

In the kitchen, Ardith said, "Your big beautiful gray cat's
a whore."

This made Muriel laugh. "What?"

"There's no doubt in my mind," Kazumi said. "He's going
to want to sleep with us."

"I can't believe he didn't hide," Muriel said. "He always
hides when there's company. Sometimes he'll show up later.
Sometimes not."

"I don't speak cat," Ardith said. "But he sounded like,
'This is my bed.'"

"It's his favorite hangout," Muriel said. "There, and in front of either woodstove."

Muriel, Kazumi, and Ardith sat down for dinner. Zachary had moved the dinner from the living room to the dining room. He was the waiter. He served them *soupe au pistou* one by one. He took a warmed-in-the-oven baguette and placed it on a long breadboard on the table. Ardith was the first to tear off a piece, then handed the loaf around. Zachary filled each of their wineglasses. He sat down, raised his glass, and said, "Happy Valentine's Day," and everyone clinked glasses.

He might have toasted the completion of Muriel's book, the end of Kazumi's semester, or Ardith's graduation, but he didn't. Muriel frowned at him in sympathy. She understood, I think, that the only personal thing he'd want himself to be congratulated for was locating Corrine Moore.

After dinner, they took their pieces of cake on plates into the living room and sat on the sofa and rockers in front of the woodstove. The stove was radiating so much heat, Zachary had turned the oil setting down to fifty-five. He made everyone an espresso. "Those maples out front are incredible," Ardith said. "Do you think they get cold in winter?"

"I've wondered that myself," Muriel said. "It's all projection, I know. But somehow, those maples don't ever look cold to me. Other trees do, though."

When they fell into a long silence, Ardith said, "When I was a little girl and this happened, my mother would always say, 'An angel is passing.'"

Conversation started up again. Then Zachary said, "Sorry, but I've got work to do. Meeting first thing in the morning." He stood up from a rocker and started up the stairs.

"We'll clean up later, darling," Muriel called out. "Dinner and dessert were perfect. I'll be up soon."

Ardith looked out at the trees, the snow-powdered dirt road, all moonlit. "My mind's never once been pastoral," she said—almost too introspective for the occasion—"but this farmhouse certainly is, Muriel. Lucky you."

After coffee, Ardith reached for another bottle of wine. She filled everyone's glass. On the sofa, Kazumi and Ardith held hands. Muriel sat across from them in a rocking chair.

I followed Zachary up to his office. He sat in his chair and listened to the playback of his recent notes.

"February eighth. I followed up on a call from a Mr. Peter Blitzer, Eight Four Six Liberty Street in Montpelier. Retired newspaper journalist, twenty-two years with the *Times Argus*. Obituary writer, occasionally reported on high school sports, some cultural stuff like concerts or movies, covered the statehouse. Now a volunteer at the Kellogg-Hubbard Library. Takes Italian classes. Widower eleven years. His wife, Paula, was in the state legislature. I had coffee with him in his kitchen. Had books everywhere, whose subjects, at a glance, were natural history and art. He's a photography buff, too.

"After fifteen or so minutes, we got to the point of my interview. He'd jotted down notes in a spiral notebook, which he set on the kitchen table. Plus—and this was a first for me—he'd actually typed out a statement. Neatly typed on white paper, with only a few whiteout smudges. I guess it's best I just read it into this tape:

On January 30 at about one o'clock I was having a sandwich and a cup of coffee in Bentley's Bakery and Café in Danville. I go there once a week and try to vary the day of the week. I had a window seat. I was the only customer. I was reading a book. A very good read.

At one point I looked out the window, and at that very instant I saw the following. In an alleyway almost directly across from the bakery was a parked car. It was dark blue but I didn't know the year or make, but it was an American car. Not vintage but not a recent year, either. Cars are not my forte. Just then the back door of the car opened and out stepped a little girl. She looked around ten or eleven, but could have been older. She wore a stocking cap drawn down enough to cover her forehead, a knee-length dark coat that seemed, at a glance, a size or two too large. She also, oddly enough, wore rain galoshes of the old sort, with buckles all the way up. Not snow boots, mind you. She stood next to the car and looked around. She seemed to be alone.

Then, all of a sudden, she reached into the car and took out a bunch of flowers and furiously tore off their petals and let them fly away in the wind all up and down the alley and onto the hood of the car. I thought, temper tantrum. I got up and went to the bathroom, and when I got back, I saw a woman somewhat roughly pick up the little girl and put her in the back seat. The little girl was flailing her arms at the woman's face. I thought, well, that happens, a child flies into a tantrum.

I didn't get a decent look at the woman, who climbed into the back seat with the girl. The car — and this was odd — backed up the alley instead of more conveniently getting into a forward gear and moving right out the few yards into the street. I sat reading awhile, had a second coffee, put on my scarf, coat, and gloves, waved so long to the bakers and a young woman behind the counter, and off I drove along Route 2 toward Montpelier. I looked over and saw the Danville post office and remembered that lying on my back seat was my quarterly income tax check, all ready to send. So I pulled up to the post office, went inside, and slid the envelope through the slot. That's when I saw Corrine Moore's face on the MISSING CHILD poster. Honestly, nothing registered until I got to Marshfield, just past Rainbow Sweets Bakery, and that's where I was hit with a thunderbolt. It hit me so hard I had to pull my car off to the side, on the road crossing over to Calais, so I could get out and vomit, which I'm sorry to say I did right there on the road. I got back into my car and drove to the Marshfield general store, and there, tacked to the front of the store near the wooden Indian, was the MISSING CHILD poster with Corrine Moore's picture on it. I studied it a long time. My gut told me one thing, my brain told me something else. I wish they would've been in agreement first thing. Agreed on the only thing of importance, for God's sake, which was that I may well have seen Corrine Moore in Danville, across from the bakery there. But a mother struggling to get her kid into the car, and maybe angry that the kid had done something petulant to boot—I mean, tearing up those flowers, how often does that sort of thing happen? Still, it kept nagging at me all the rest of the afternoon, until I said to myself, You could regret not doing it, so you better call the police and the investigator you read about in the *Times Argus* at the Green Mountain Agency. Of which I did both.

"I went over things with Peter Blitzer again and again, no stone unturned, and I could see he was quite torn up. He said, 'The problem with this kind of situation is that a familiar sight, a little girl giving her mother a tough time, should just be a familiar sight and nothing so sinister as part of a kidnapping, right? But what with the posters everywhere you look, it can't be just familiar, can it?' I knew what he meant, and said I did.

"I pressed him once more: 'Are you sure you can't remember more about the car, for instance? And let me ask you this. If we hired an old-fashioned police sketch artist, do you think you might remember the woman's face in more detail?' Blitzer shook his head. He looked so overwrought, I felt I had to leave him be.

"The next morning, in blowing snow but the roads passable, I drove to Danville. I sat by the window in Bentley's Bakery and Café and looked across to the alley. I had coffee and a blueberry muffin, then walked toward the alley. I went into a thrift shop next to the alley and asked the owner, a Mrs. Perry, a bunch of questions and showed her a photograph of Corrine. I asked her opinion as to what rhyme or reason the car might've been parked in the alley. Did she remember, at the time of day Mr. Blitzer mentioned, a woman customer? Or a male customer, for that matter, since the woman in question had gotten into the back seat, so perhaps a man had backed the car up, or it might have been another woman, did Mrs. Perry have any knowledge of any of this? But she didn't. Mrs. Perry said, 'Yesterday I did have two customers. But they are both high school girls I have known since they were children.' I wrote down their names and the directions to their houses, which Mrs. Perry knew by heart.

"I immediately visited both high school girls—first Binnie Persons, then Mary Beth Singleton—on the outside chance that either or both might've noticed something pertinent, but they hadn't. I drove back to the bakery. It was almost dusk now. I walked back to the alley. I looked down and found some trampled flower petals. I put those in the breast pocket of my shirt. Then I noticed a flower petal that appeared to be pasted to the outside wall of the thrift shop. I peeled that petal off and put it in the same pocket. I drove back to Montpelier and went to Petals and Things, the flower shop on Main Street, across from the fire station. Weekdays they're open until seven. I spoke with a florist named Kelly Shrift. I showed her my ID and said I was investigating the missing child case of Corrine Moore. 'Oh, my God,' she said. 'I have been praying for her. My whole church has.'

"On the glass counter, I laid out the petals from the alley in Danville. 'Can you tell me what flower these come from?'

"With the tip of a pencil she separated out the petal I'd peeled from the alley wall. 'There's only this one I can work with,' she said.

"Kelly then took out a catalog of flowers and flower arrangements. Paging through it, she settled on a page of orchids. She moved the chosen petal down the column. 'Here it is,' she said. 'It's what's called a Lovely Lavender Orchid.' She matched it up and showed me the illustration. Definitely, that was the right flower. I asked if there was a copy machine in the office, and she said yes. I asked if she'd copy the page with the Lovely Lavender Orchid on it, which she did right away. I took her business card, said thanks, and gave her my agency card. 'You've been a great help,' I said. 'I hope so,' she said, 'because prayers haven't worked yet.'

"I put the petal in a small plastic bag. Then I drove to the office and added the photocopied page to the file, and copied *that* on the office machine for my duplicate file. I spoke with Mr. Vlamick. I told him my report files were where they always were, on my desk. I drove home. End of report."

AT ABOUT ELEVEN O'CLOCK, Zachary took a shower, put two new logs in the bedroom's woodstove, and got under the bedclothes. He lay there listening to the voices drifting up. I went down to sit in the library. From the tenor of the conversation in the living room, I suspected that Muriel, Valentine's Day or not, Zachary waiting in bed for her or not, had no intention of going upstairs quite yet.

The talk was raucous, intimate, argumentative, intense. Subject-wise, a bit all over the place. Then they began to discuss a poem by Mukei Korin, apparently the final one to appear in Muriel's book, which did not appear in her dissertation. "Let me read the entire poem as I now have it," Muriel said.

> The scarecrow invites the crows for tea.
> Sipping tea on their porch, the farmer and his wife
> watch the proceedings. (If I place my hand here on your body, you move
>   it to a preferable place, there is urgent agreement.)
> The farmer says, "Maybe I gave the scarecrow
> too welcoming a nature."

*His wife says, "You worked long hours on it
and that is how it turned out."*

"Let's talk about what's inside the parentheses, shall we?" Kazumi said. They all laughed, and Kazumi said, "I'll start, okay? I like very much the phrase 'urgent agreement.'"

"Yes, but it's pretty euphemistic," Ardith said.

"Euphemistic for what?" Muriel asked.

"I think Ardith is implying she can offer an alternative," Kazumi said.

"How about, 'we came at the same time'?" Ardith said.

"Hardly befitting of our poet's sense of decorum," Muriel said.

"Decorum or repression," Ardith said. "But I'd have to defer to Kazumi, to how the original Japanese reads."

In the course of the next half hour, the single phrase, as Muriel had construed it — *there is urgent agreement* — was taken apart, put together, linguistically refracted, and debated for and against, against and for. Muriel referred to "idiomatic nuance." To say the least, the erudition, let alone the level of engagement with particulars, was impressive, which would be no surprise to Zachary. He'd heard Muriel and Kazumi holding similarly analytical discussions many times, both on the telephone and in person. What's more, the equal contributions from Ardith I imagined served to deepen the connection between her and Kazumi. Scholarship as a form of courtship, it seemed to me.

"I think it was five or so years ago," Kazumi said, "I was dating a guy named Anthony Folder. Dr. Tony Folder, and he taught economics at a community college. And one

night after dinner out, we went back to his house in Portsmouth, an ocean view. Somehow or other, our clothes fell
to the floor."

"'Somehow,'" Ardith said.

"And we were sitting on an overstuffed chair," Kazumi
continued. "The bed was nearby, but we, for some reason,
stayed on the chair. I was on his lap, and we were faced in the
same direction."

"Ocean view?" Ardith said.

"As a matter of fact, yes. He placed his hand on my knee,
and I moved it to a preferable place. Some lovely moments
of expertise, and then urgent agreement, except just between me and myself, his hand along for the ride."

Much groaning laughter, until Muriel stood and said,
"Thanks, ladies, for all the close attention to literary matters.
And for urgent agreement, that my original word choices
were best. And above all, I'm glad it brought back such fond
memories for Kazumi. I'm off to dreamland. There's more
of everything in the fridge. Enjoy. See you in the morning.
First one up makes coffee, please."

Muriel walked past me on the stairs and went into her
and Zachary's bedroom. Zachary had tempered the woodstove's heat by propping open a window a little with a book.
He was under the bedclothes, wearing his Lenny Bruce T-
shirt, with the words TRUTH CAN KILL YOU, BUT IT'S BETTER
THAN LIVING A LIE. Muriel took a brief shower and emerged
from the bathroom wearing a robe. She was drying her hair
in furious eddies with a bath towel. "I'm half asleep," Zachary said.

"I got caught up in a little shop talk with the girls," Muriel said. "It's only a few minutes past Valentine's Day, though."

She let the bathrobe fall away to the floor, then slid under the bedclothes. They kissed deeply, and Zachary placed his hands on her hips. She moved his left hand to a preferable place. I walked down to the library.

THE NEXT MORNING, Ardith was first to the kitchen. She made coffee, put a log in the woodstove, stirred up the coals, and the log flared. It was snowing heavily. Soon Kazumi came down, followed by Muriel. When the three of them sat together in the living room, each with a mug, Kazumi said, "Muriel, my love, was there urgent agreement last night?"

"I could ask you the same question, but I won't."

"Ardith makes killer french toast," Kazumi said.

"May I use your kitchen?" Ardith asked.

"All the accoutrements are in plain sight," Muriel said. "Maple syrup's in the fridge, bottom shelf. Brown sugar's above the microwave."

Ardith went into the kitchen. Zachary came downstairs, dressed for work. He moved with haste to the kitchen, said, "Oh, there's coffee, thanks," poured himself a mug, set it on the counter, threw on his winter coat, slipped on his gloves, picked up the mug, and said, "I'm late, sweetheart."

Muriel hurried in to kiss him goodbye. "I'll be here all day," she said. "Though I might take the ladies out on snow-shoes."

"Me, on snowshoes?" Kazumi said.

Zachary was out the mudroom door and into his pickup in a moment's time.

Standing in the kitchen doorway, Muriel said, "This missing girl case — Corrine Moore, age eleven. It's turned Zach inside out."

I went out to my cabin and the hours passed. It was well after dark — it got dark at 4:30 in February — before I returned to the house. I'd been listening to CBC radio and hypothesizing why I didn't feel in the least cold, considering the propane stove wasn't turned on. I also spent what I might call hypnotized hours, simply staring at snow on the branches of the crabapple trees near the cabin.

When I returned to the farmhouse, Kazumi, Ardith, and Muriel were dishing out leftover *soupe au pistou.* There was half a loaf of bread, and wine, and ice water in a pitcher. I noticed the table was set for four.

But Zachary didn't show up for dinner. Dishes were cleared by nine, coffee followed, and when everyone was sitting in the living room again, sipping small, narrow glasses of limoncello, Muriel said, "Really, it's not like Zach not to call. He's never once missed dinner, at least without calling. Since we've moved to this house, not once." The three of them went up to watch a movie on the television in the guest room.

About eleven o'clock, the phone rang. Muriel went into the master bedroom and picked up. "I've been worried sick." She listened a moment, then said, "Well, all right, Mrs. Moore. I don't completely understand, but I appreciate your calling." She set the phone down. She had to compose herself a moment before returning to the movie.

But in the doorway she said, "Going to bed."

"What's up with Zachary?" Kazumi asked. "He's okay, right?"

"Sweet dreams," Muriel said.

She went back to her bedroom, closed the door, got into her cotton pajamas, climbed into bed. She read a few pages of *Snow Country* by Yasunari Kawabata, then turned off the bedside lamp.

ZACHARY TELEPHONED AT 8 the next morning, but didn't return home until 6:30 p.m., by which time Kazumi and Ardith had no doubt already arrived back in Portsmouth. Muriel had prepared a salad with ingredients purchased at the Adamant co-op: arugula, cherry tomatoes, carrots, scallions, and stalks of asparagus, which she'd sautéed, seasoned with oregano, and set in a latticework over the salad. She favored the raw and cooked combination in her salads of late. She had prepared an oil and vinegar dressing, with two squeezes of lemon. There was more than enough Valentine cake left for dessert.

When Zachary stepped into the house, he right away said, "I know we have to talk." He and Muriel were people who tried to look right at life. Both hated to allow civility to become avoidance, at least as far as I could tell. Zachary took off his coat and threw it across a kitchen chair. He then walked in to sit at the table Muriel had set. The salad was in a big wooden bowl; the wooden serving utensils were balanced rim to rim. "I'm sorry," he said, sitting down.

Muriel came up behind Zachary and hugged him, kissed

his face, and said, "I feel like crying, but it's mainly from worry and not sleeping. Remember what your mother used to say, may she rest: 'Life will provide. Life will be fine, if not peachy.' Generally, it's a good philosophy, I guess. We, you and I, are fine, Zach. But last night wasn't all that peachy. We do have to talk."

Muriel sat down across from him. They each served themselves dinner. Muriel held her wineglass in the air, Zachary followed suit, and she said, "To figuring things out." They clinked glasses and each took a sip of wine. "Please tell me why you felt the need to stay at the Moores' house overnight. I worried it had to do with feeling left out on Valentine's Day and everything."

"Come on, Muriel, I love it when you get so deep into your literary subjects with Kazumi. I've always loved it. I'm dying to know what you think of Ardith, too. It's very nice, Kazumi being so trusting of your friendship. My staying at the Moores' had nothing to do with that."

"Are you sure, Zach?"

"I think so, yes. Tell me, were you embarrassed, what with us having guests, that I didn't come home? Did they ask about it?"

"I'd say they were discreet, Zach. None of that matters, though. What the hell is going on? Just tell me."

"I don't know what happened, exactly."

"Just go chronologically, maybe you'll find out. I hardly slept a wink. You owe it to me."

"I had a long day, mainly meetings and paperwork. Two hours reviewing with the state police. No good leads, nothing. It hasn't been in the newspaper yet, but late last night a body was found in the Winooski River. I was told this by the state police, and it wasn't for four more hours till I learned it wasn't Corrine. How can it come to this, Murr? That I was relieved—even happy, I have to admit it—that someone other than Corrine Moore drowned. I hardly recognized myself."

"I'm so sorry."

"Don't feel sorry for me, please. I'm not complaining. No violins. I'm just going through it chronologically, like you said."

"Go on."

"Then I was cornered by a reporter for the *Burlington Free Press.* He wanted to base a whole article on the phenomenon of false leads. That's how he put it, 'the phenomenon of false leads.' He seemed to think it was a witty concept. A good hook. He was very aggressive. I kind of lost my cool, end of the day. My comportment did not reflect well on my chosen profession, let me put it that way. I got to the Moores' house about seven. I'd called ahead to say I needed to speak with them. But the truth was, I had nothing planned to say. Not really."

"Zach, you didn't call me all day."

"I wasn't aware of not calling."

"That makes it worse. But no matter. Continue."

"In their house, there's photographs of Corrine every-where."

"They're living a nightmare."

"Something happened. It was very disturbing."

"Tell me."

"The phone rang, and it was someone saying she'd seen

Corrine at the Star Theater in St. Johnsbury. 'It's another sighting,' Johanna said and handed me the phone. I identified myself and the woman said the name of the movie, the time, where Corrine was sitting, all sorts of details. I interrupted and said, 'Give me your name and address, please. I'll come by to talk with you in person. It's procedure.' She slammed down the phone. Johanna then took out a yellow legal pad, and it was full, page after page of this kind of call. I was flabbergasted, Murr. Just flabbergasted. I could hardly breathe. I rudely insisted that they give me that legal pad right now, right now! I sort of grabbed it from Johanna and she looked startled. I flipped through five or six pages, all useless nonsense. Those poor people."

"And you now have to follow up on every name on that legal pad. Of course you do."

"I lost my temper."

"I imagine they asked you to stay for dinner."

"Yes. And I should've called you. They needed to talk about their daughter. At dinner this thing was said by Devon. It really got to me. I'd read in the report how Corrine liked to gently lift moths from her neighbors' walls first thing in the morning."

"You told me. I remember that. I couldn't forget that."

"But naturally that's confined to summer, right? Moths are only in summer."

"Once in a while I find one still fluttering around in, what, January or February. This old farmhouse is hospitable to that."

"But in the main."

"Yes, of course. Moths are only in summer."

"Johanna sets down chicken and rice, and then Devon falls apart, right at the table. His plate falls to the floor. Their dog comes right over. Johanna helps her husband up and takes him into their bedroom. I clear away the plate that fell. When she comes back, Johanna says, 'There's no moths in winter. What's Corrine doing every day? Where is she? Who has her? What's she doing? Is she getting her baths? She doesn't like the water too hot. She dropped her field guide near the co-op, you remember? What's she going to do without it?'"

Zachary was beyond upset now, and Muriel reached across and held his wrist, and said, "Zach, it's okay."

"I'm a train wreck. I'm maybe not cut out for this."

"No, that's not true."

"Mr. Vlamick has put Erica fully on the case now."

"That just means it requires it. I'm glad to hear this, Zach. You're very good at what you do. But you can't do it alone. Not this time. Not with Corrine."

"I don't know anymore."

"So, you stayed for dinner. I get that. But why stay over?"

"Here's how that happened. It'll sound lame, but it's what happened. Johanna—this was when Devon came back to the table—she brought out some dessert. Homemade brownies. She says, 'My husband and I have stepped up our own investigation. We have to be . . . hands-on. Otherwise we'll go completely mad.' Right then and there I asked if they'd been going to the homes of anyone on the legal pad, anyone who volunteered their address. Total silence. So I think the answer is yes. I really do. All I could do was explain how dangerous that could be. At which point, Johanna says,

'Zachary, you and your wife Muriel don't have children yet, right?' I said that was true. And she says, 'Then you can't really understand.' There was this horrible silence for about five minutes, then Johanna finally says, 'My husband and I don't think our daughter is dead. We think we'd know if she was. We'd just know.' Then Johanna suggests that we sit in the living room.

"Devon brought out a bottle of cherry liqueur. 'You might look at me and not think I'd be the type for this stuff, but now and then it hits the spot,' he says. 'Thanks for calling and coming to see us so often. It's been much appreciated. But this whole situation, it's gotten so horrible, it's tempting us to become spiritual people, and we aren't spiritual people. A lot of proselytizers—I don't know what else to call them—a lot have rung our doorbell, and they want to give us spiritual guidance, as to how to live through what we're living through. We try to slam the door in a polite fashion.' He poured us each a snifter of the liqueur. Johanna passed on it. 'But you can't contrive faith,' she says. I started to sip some of the liqueur, and Murr, it was the last thing I remember. I knew I was exhausted, but . . . Anyway, I woke on the sofa about six in the morning and drove right to the office."

"You didn't drive home."

"I drove to the office."

"You do definitely look totally exhausted, Zach. You spent the whole day at the office, right? But at least you called this morning. I took a nap right away after you called."

"I was so homesick today. Just half an hour's drive, but completely homesick. I made bad decisions. I was all bad decisions."

"That sounds a little woe-is-me, feeling all sorry for myself. Unlike you."

"I'd like to go upstairs and sleep now."

"Zach, you know what? Around eleven last night, Johanna Moore called here. She told me you'd fallen asleep on their sofa. She'd said if I wanted, she'd wake you up and drive you home. I told her just to let you sleep."

"But you still wanted me to explain things. I understand. Why wouldn't you?"

"I'll go up with you, Zach. You can fall asleep to my opinion about Ardith Paleo."

BIRD AND
BREAKING WAVE

L ONG AFTER Muriel and Zachary went to bed, at three
o'clock in the morning, I noticed, in my cabin, a photograph of Lorca and me on the beach north of Point Reyes,
California. It could only have been taken in the summer of
1987, because that's the only time we were there together—
it was the tenth year of our marriage. In the photograph,
Lorca was dressed in a T-shirt, sweater draped around her
shoulders, shorts, and flip-flops. She held a surf-casting pole
in one hand, and a good-sized blue perch dangled from the
thumb of the other hand. She looked quite proud of herself. In fact, she was beaming. Back in the fourth year of our
marriage, 1981, we were settled nicely in the farmhouse. One
night in bed, Lorca said, "It's not that we haven't been trying—or should I say, we haven't been cautious. But now I
think it's really time, Simon. To give it all our—"

"Attentions," I said.

"—heart and soul."

We both very much wanted a child. It was equal, there was
no hesitation, we both felt it would be a wonderful reprieve

from thinking about ourselves, every other good thing. I'd sold a screenplay for what struck us as more than decent money. I put away some of the salary from a visiting professorship—one semester—at UC Santa Cruz, though I flew back to Vermont every two weeks, which was pricey. Lorca's most recent exhibition of drawings and paintings, at Gallery NAGA in Boston, had sold out (miracles never cease), and the mortgage on our farmhouse continued to prove manageable. We paid our income taxes in full, the property tax in increments.

All of this gave us the confidence that we could support a child. Of course, we knew life could suddenly intervene, life was provisional, life was this or that. We knew that my second novel had done little in sales. We also knew, despite Lorca's astonishing gift, that the art market was dubious at best. Still, the conversations day and night, the desire, the comfort in recognizing we wanted a child, the private joy simply in the wanting, were all present and accounted for. And so we tried. And sometimes we tried, as Lorca said, by the book.

We tried, and there were two consecutive miscarriages. Like the many women who had suffered a miscarriage, Lorca heard, from two different physicians, "At least you know you can get pregnant. It sometimes takes a while." The body is quite capable of trafficking in false encouragement, though, and after the second miscarriage, Lorca said, "I'm not failing you, am I, Simon?" "No one's failing anyone," I said. This kind of conversation was not a matter of logical progression, of probity with a clear understanding at the end, no, not that kind of conversation at all, but of just feeling miserable. Look, I know there are books written about how a miscarriage engenders a sense of grief. You start to think one way about life, you might even discuss whom to name your child after, and suddenly you have to think a completely other way about life — and it can begin to torment you, or become for both of you a duet of torment, and by that I mean you can feel you're being punished for something, but you can't know what. And, of course, on the physical, let alone emotional, level, I couldn't fully comprehend how Lorca registered it all. She had ways of talking about it, but they were ways that always ended in tears.

We knew we were hardly alone in all of this. In fact, we attended a support group — not like us to do such a thing, but we did it anyway. It was held in the Quaker meeting house in Montpelier. The group leader said an interesting thing: "No matter what your religious faith, in our meeting house the loss of a child is considered nondenominational grief. It's simply human grief." The ten or fifteen couples that always showed up, mainly we talked among ourselves. "Goddamn it to hell, I'm just going to say it," one regular attendee said one evening. "I love all of you, but it's like belonging to a club you never wanted to belong to."

We had appointments at three different fertility clinics. I gave Lorca fertility shots on a strict schedule. We consulted far and wide. She continued to paint, I continued to write, but this was our real preoccupation. Lorca marked calendars; she took her temperature. "Now would be a good time. Let's go to bed." We began to feel it was our full-time job and secret identity, us, this couple, this writer, this painter, who loved sleeping together, who had a deep physical attraction, who made love in the kitchen ("Wow — just because the espresso was so good?"), the guest bedrooms, of course our bedroom. In the bathtub—well, once. Quite often on the sofa in the library; we just swept the books aside.

Fifteen months after the second miscarriage, we gathered funds, found a house sitter (a painter friend from Lorca's RISD days), and flew out to San Francisco. We rented a car and drove to Inverness. There, we stayed in a cottage owned by the Holly Tree Inn. We had some clothes, books, binoculars. Lorca brought her sketchbooks, but really, that was it. We pared down and left the farmhouse. We didn't have a cat yet. The cottage was on stilts, at the end of a dock that stretched out into Tomales Bay. Walking on its differently warped slats was like walking on a long wooden xylophone; you felt you'd composed a jazz riff just by leaving or returning on foot. The cottage itself was pretty basic fare. One large room, a kitchen area, a bath, a bedroom, and an upstairs library with a wide desk and gooseneck lamp. Depending on the strength and direction, the breeze often delivered the scent of eucalyptus, or brine. Late afternoons and early evenings, ospreys, often with a fish clutched in their talons, would fly over the cottage, close enough so that we could see their fierce eyes and the tilting calibrations of their wings. In the morning, Lorca and I woke to the sound of ducks muttering beneath the cottage. We learned that the cottage had once been owned by a member of Frank Zappa's band, the Mothers of Invention. In a drawer, we found a Zappa album, *Lumpy Gravy,* and we played it a lot. There was an old phonograph, with two extra needles Scotch-taped to the side. We also found jazz albums, opera, rock-and-roll, classical, Tex-Mex.

We talked about it and decided that a routine, though with lots of room for delinquency, would be good. So, first thing in the morning we'd drive over to Point Reyes Station, sit with our bear claws and coffee on the bench outside a local bakery. We would then browse in Point Reyes Books, after which we'd cross the street to the Palace Market, where we'd buy green plums, grapes, sandwiches, and bottled water. Then we'd drive out to the Estero Trail in the Point Reyes National Seashore, or to Limantour Beach, or to horseshoe-shaped McClures Beach, which was a walk down a steep path from Pierce Point Ranch. My favorite was McClures Beach; there were always pelicans. Lorca had her sketchbooks in a backpack; she was attempting landscapes. We had a routine. We needed a routine.

Late evenings, back from dinner in town, or after a sunset walk at Limantour, we were always in the cottage. Because, in a sense, the world arrived to the cottage, or all the world we could handle. The stars, the tide, the seabirds and shorebirds, the moon, books to read, the radio. We did love our life in Vermont, but we needed to be away from it. In town, we began to recognize a few faces, especially in the market, the bookstore, or the bakery. But we didn't try to make friends. We didn't seek invitations. We needed to think things through. Not necessarily think things through in conversation, but think things through nonetheless. We found ourselves sleeping at odd hours.

One thing about our three months in the cottage that surprised us: our newly discovered devotion to surf-casting. We never could've predicted this. On a hot, still afternoon, along a stretch of beach north of the official border of the national seashore, we saw a Japanese-American man, woman, and three children, each holding a long pole, surf-casting at intervals of roughly ten yards from one another. Each had a bucket full, we saw when we eventually walked over, of squid for bait. The children, at closest guess, were a boy of fifteen, a girl around twelve, and a girl of seven or eight. They wielded their poles deftly. They shared two transistor radios between them.

After an hour or so of watching them, Lorca went up and spoke to the wife—at first, of course, we didn't know the exact family configuration, but it turned out we were right, they were indeed a family—and I could see immediately that it was an animated conversation. Then Lorca waved me over.

Lorca asked straight out if they'd teach us how to surf-cast. By now the whole family had gathered, though they had left their poles fixed to the beach, the baited hooks out in the surf, bells attached to the lines should there be a strike. "You must've only arrived a short time ago," Lorca said, "because there's no fish in your buckets or ice chests."

The entire family broke up laughing, and the father said, "No, actually, we've been here many hours. Just no luck as of yet."

"I see," Lorca said.

"This is a good beach for blue perch," the mother said. "And sand sharks."

"I read where sand sharks have to be thrown back," Lorca said.

"Every fish wants to be thrown back," the father said.

"I see," Lorca said.

The mother introduced the family, and we introduced ourselves. Then their son, Kai, walked back to his pole, carrying a transistor radio.

"Kai is the best fisherman in our family," the mother, Keiko, said. "He seems to believe that it has something to do with the radio station he listens to. He sometimes hangs the radio from his fishing pole."

The daughters were named Azami and Asa, the father was Akihiko. "However," Asa, the youngest daughter, said, "I have caught the biggest fish any one of us has caught, including before I was born, correct?"

"That is correct," her father said. "But lately we don't necessarily benefit from Kai's fishing skills. Or let us say, we aren't the first beneficiaries."

"He has a serious girlfriend," Asa said.

"I heard that!" Kai shouted. He turned up his radio and hung it high up on his pole.

"I'm wondering if you'd teach my husband and me to surf-cast," Lorca said.

This surprised me. But I said, "Yes, you see, I'm not very good at anything like this."

"Why not sit on the beach here, close by?" Keiko said. "Just watch us. Then, in a half hour or so, you can try it out for yourselves."

"That sounds great," Lorca said.

Kai was off in his own world, but the rest of the family each reeled in their lines, made sure we were paying attention, and baited their hooks with new squid. Then, one by one, they cast far out into the ocean. They secured each pole to the beach, then sat in fold-up chairs with cloth backings. Keiko soon dozed off.

Lorca said to Azami, "Would your parents allow us to pay for our lesson? I'd like to do that."

Azami said, "They would say no to that kind offer. But if you give me and my sister each a dollar, we would tell our parents about it later, and the next day, they'd make us try to find you on this beach to return it. But if we can't find you, we'll use the money for squid, and that will make it almost all right. Our father will say his favorite proverb: Even the thief has practical concerns."

"Wow, you have it all thought out," Lorca said.

"I always have everything thought out," Azami said, laughing. "And sometimes what I think out actually comes true." She had a wonderful laugh.

Lorca slipped Azami two one-dollar bills. Azami immediately looked to see if her father was observing; he was looking out to sea. He had sunglasses on. Azami ran to her sister, handed her one of the bills, then ran back to her chair and sat down.

Lorca was the first to try out a pole, Keiko's, as it turned out. First Keiko demonstrated how to properly attach the squid bait, then the reach back and arc of the cast. Lorca pantomimed a cast a couple of times, and then let fly. The line, perhaps at a little too horizontal a trajectory, landed far out in the water, and Lorca right away had an expectant look, as if a fish might've already risen to the bait.

"Now, set the pole in the holder on the beach," Keiko said. "Sit down and think of something to think about. When I sit, I like to think of my children's early days, especially when we lived in Monterey, where they were born."

It was my turn, and I used Kai's pole, as he wanted to take a walk up the beach. "Keep the radio tuned to the jazz station out of Oakland," he said, "or else you'll catch only sand sharks." As he started off on his walk, he took out a cigarette and kissed his mother on top of her head, to me an interesting combination of gestures. My first cast sent the line almost parallel to the beach, where the bait landed with a splat.

"Mr. Simon," Keiko said, "thank you for feeding a seagull." And sure enough, in swooped a big seagull and nabbed the piece of squid and flew off with it. "We like to have a good relationship with all the birds along this beach."

Lorca and I cast several more times each, until Akihiko said, "We have to try and catch some future dinners now."

He informed us that his brother, in fact, owned a sporting goods store in San Rafael with a big inventory of surf-casting poles. He also told us the best place to buy squid was the seafood stand in Stinson Beach. "Just ask, anyone there will know it," he said.

The next morning, we drove to San Rafael and purchased two St. Croix surf-casting poles. We bought two sets of five hooks each. Then we drove to Stinson Beach to find the roadside stand, and found it easily, and purchased twenty squid there. We already had a bucket we'd found in the storage space of the cottage. In Point Reyes Station we bought rain slickers.

We were definitely bumblers at the art of surf-casting; early on, our casts fed many seagulls. We nonetheless had fortitude. We went to the same beach every day, late in the afternoon. In the main, if we caught anything, it was a sand shark. Or a blue perch of modest size, which we let go. Within a week, Lorca had purchased a transistor radio, which she tuned to the Oakland jazz station, and fastened the radio to her pole, just above the handle. And, lo and behold, on the first afternoon she did that, she caught a very large — at least in our estimation — blue perch, which is what the photograph showed. That perch we cooked using a recipe we found while browsing used and new cookbooks in Point Reyes Books.

The logistics of surf-casting proved very useful to us — in our marriage, I mean. Because surf-casting requires that two people stand in parallel alignment, both, of course, facing the sea. So Lorca and I would stand roughly ten yards from each other. Close enough so that if the wind didn't swallow our voices, we could talk, and concentrate on whatever was the subject at hand, all the while unconsciously alert to the vibration along our poles, and to the seabirds and shorebirds, the seals, the light glinting off the water, even the occasional behemoth freighter making its way — moving without moving, it often seemed — across the horizon. And we talked openly, but didn't have to read, or possibly misread, each other's expressions, because either might prove ruinous.

We had a giant umbrella fixed to the hard sand, a cooler full of bottled water, prosecco, sandwiches, and green and purple plums. We had a bucket of squid. We had extra hooks and sinkers in a black tackle box.

Our increasing skill at casting had no discernible effect on our luck. The most gorgeously arcing cast might bring in a blue perch, but more than likely it wouldn't. The plaintive cries of plovers. Pelicans, gulls. Bird and breaking wave, bird and breaking wave. Sanderlings racing along, poking and prodding, as if attempting with their bills to stitch the darkly spreading hem of a wave to the beach before it sank away into the sand. Like stitching the end of the sea and the end of the land together. The thrill of not knowing what creature was on the end of the line until it was reeled in. The permanent rictus grins of sand sharks, the amazement at how sandpapery their skin was, the fact that they emitted guttural cries and would so powerfully writhe and snap the air, even the smallest of them, the urgent need to survive. And we stayed late some evenings, the squid bait beckoning out in moonlit dark waters. Nothing, nothing, nothing in the universe for hours on end save for the sound of the ocean and the stars. Lorca said on one such evening, "How many times have you or I said, 'Hey, is that a planet?'" For some reason, this made us laugh.

Three or four times, we stayed on the beach all night. The breeze set off false alarms in the two bells attached to the lines. The surprise that gulls flew nocturnally. On the transistor radio, an oldies station out of San Rafael, or that jazz channel from Oakland with the cool, super-hip deejays, classical out of San Francisco, this or that, depending on the whims of reception. Once in a while, the classical station would suddenly become rock-and-roll, sometimes for only ten or fifteen minutes, then return to classical. Lorca liked to blame seagulls for this phenomenon. There was something unsettling about seagulls for her. Pelicans were another story altogether; she loved to watch them float in armadas just offshore or fly in a regimented line low to the water, and she sketched a number of these, too. Thermoses of coffee. Mangoes and tangerines. Limes for the vodka. Around midnight we'd slip bulky sweaters on. Next day after dawn—such magnificent sunrises—rain slickers beaded with cold mist, we'd pack up and drive to the cottage, and fall into bed next to each other in our squid-smelling clothes.

It happened that, a week before we had to leave the cottage, Lorca and I each caught a midsized perch, which we brought back and baked so that the drippings soaked into the sliced potatoes underneath. We had a salad and an expensive bottle of Italian wine, and afterward we sat on the veranda and talked late into the night. Lorca was quite certain that was the night she became pregnant again.

A year or so later, Lorca said, "I knew at the time it was a mistake to name her. But I sort of felt it helped us both to name her." She was referring to the fact that, in the third month of her pregnancy, we'd found out we were going to have a girl, and had agreed to give her the name Hattie, after Lorca's beloved maternal grandmother. But early in the fourth month, Lorca lost Hattie—we lost her—and I can scarcely describe it. We fell apart. We didn't leave the farmhouse for nearly a month, except to shop for food. We watched movies half the night and hardly slept the other half. We cooked elaborate meals that went uneaten. On the drive back from a follow-up appointment with Lorca's doctor, we went to Bear Pond Books and bought twenty-five novels, mostly paperbacks, no doubt with the intention of filling our inner lives with other people's lives. We didn't read a single one of them, though we did read *A Grief Observed* by C. S. Lewis — an author neither of us could stand before or since — which was about the death of his wife, but about grieving in general, too. We bought tapes to learn Italian, scrupulously did the lessons, and never once used a word of Italian with each other in the house. One morning I found the *Times Argus* in the freezer compartment of our refrigerator, but I didn't mention it to Lorca. That month, my entire writing life consisted of nothing. Lorca had by that time permanently taken over the rooms above the Adamant co-op as her studio, but during the period I'm referring to, she drove over there only once, and was back home within the hour. To put it simply, things got far worse before they got the least bit better. After the loss of Hattie, we slept only in the afternoons for, if I remember correctly, more than four months. That thing about disappointments being in direct relation to expectations? Well, for Lorca and me, as far as conceiving was concerned, we now allowed ourselves no expectations, none. You might've thought, going by the received equation, this would mean no future disappointments, but it only really meant exhaustive past disappointments were fully resident in the house with us, seemingly without cease, for a very long time.

Perhaps it's odd to think back on our time in Inverness, all these years later. You can't much help where your mind goes. Yet I remember the only other time we saw that Japanese-American family. It had to be at least a month after we'd first encountered them. Our second meeting was on the same beach. Lorca and I had fallen asleep in the late-afternoon sun on a blanket between our two fishing poles stuck in the sand. When we woke, it was to a fog so thick we could hear but not see the water. The beach was all spectral atmosphere. We could hear but not see gulls. "Brrrr," Lorca said. "We'll catch our death. I didn't know it could get this foggy just like that." We threw on sweaters, then rain slickers, started to pack up our picnic basket, draw in the fishing lines, and so on. When I was tying off the hook to the end of my pole, I heard a radio, intermittent static and music. The sound, while I couldn't quite tell which direction it was coming from, seemed to be getting closer. Then, suddenly — and I mean as if materializing right out of the cold fog — there was Azami, a transistor radio in one hand, and in the other she held two one-dollar bills, which she folded into my rain slicker pocket.

"I see you and your wife didn't catch any fish," she said. "My whole family — we were a ways down the beach. We waved but you didn't see us. We caught three fish." And just like that, she started to jump, like she was playing hopscotch, then ran a short way, at which point I glimpsed, or thought I did, the rest of her family waiting for her. But almost immediately they disappeared into the fog. I could hear radio static and laughter, and then both faded and were gone.

I went to tell Lorca what had just happened. But when I reached her, she was shivering.

"Let's go now, Simon," she said. "Please. I'm really cold. We've got that Stoli in the fridge, remember?"

I never did tell her about Azami's sudden appearance and disappearance. I don't know why I didn't, but I didn't.

A WEEK AFTER Valentine's Day, as they were getting
ready for bed, Zachary said to Muriel, "I'm starting to
look at ten or twenty people a day — just on the street in
town, or driving past them in their cars — as possible kidnappers."

"Not good," Muriel said. "It's not paranoid, but it's not
natural, either. Sort of hallucinating everyday life or something. What do you think you can do to change it, Zach?"

"When I told Erica this was happening, she said, 'Welcome
to the fucked-up part of the profession.' She also said, the
only thing is to keep to procedure. And try to sleep more
than the three hours a night I've been sleeping. The less
sleep, the more clouded one's judgment."

"You slept a good five hours last night."

"So you noticed, huh?"

"Zachary, come on. Of course I noticed. I notice when
you come to bed. I notice when you leave the bed. And, despite all the stresses and strains, I more than notice when
you're in bed, right?"

"I never thought so much about parentheses."

"Me neither. And I wrote a whole damn dissertation on them."

"Murr, you are a very beautiful, very sexy, and very irresistible woman."

"Tell me."

"You are a very beautiful, very sexy, and completely irresistible woman."

"From 'very' to 'completely.' Now I believe you."

"So why do you have such a serious expression all of a sudden?"

"Because. I'm going to say something to you, sweetheart. It has to do with—crudely put, with fucking as often as we want. Making love, I mean, keeping that part of our life strongly present. I mean, it occurred to me, and this was just last week. It *frightened* me, a thought I had."

"Which thought was that?"

"My thought was that somewhere deep in that complicated mind of yours, you might be afraid—afraid of wanting to have a child with me. Because, what with Corrine's situation. What with your deep sympathies with Johanna and Devon."

"So, Murr, your thought was what? That knowing what can happen to a child in the world? Seeing how it's torn her parents to pieces. That I would feel, *what if that happened to us?*"

"That's pretty much it."

Zachary said, "If I recognized that was happening, I'd quit this job on the spot. Pick up the phone and say, 'I quit.' Muriel, I love you, and I am very, very sorry that all of this has even put that thought into your head. I love this work, and I hate what's happened to that little girl."

"I hate it, too."

"And neither of us could've foreseen any of this. Like that Robert Frost line you're always quoting——"

"'The best way out is always through.'"

"I'm in full partnership mode with Erica now."

"I do think that's for the best."

From what I could hear as I sat in the library, Epilogue draped across the typewriter, Muriel and Zachary scarcely slept that night, but not out of worry or preoccupation, but (as the writer Jean Rhys put it, far better than I could) entwined together in trust.

A FULL TWO WEEKS LATER, after a night of returning to the sore subject of Zachary's sleep patterns and all of what they implied, Muriel announced that she had to stay in Durham for five days, in part for a faculty retreat and in part for individual meetings in her office with senior honors students, mainly to determine their thesis topics, as a thesis was a requirement for graduation. The Monday morning Muriel was to leave, Zachary lingered at breakfast, and it was sweetly disciplined against all natural tendencies how they both seemed to be calibrating every sentence to avoid any subject they wouldn't have time, then and there, to talk through.

I want to chronicle this week when Muriel was away from the farmhouse, because so much of import took place then. Naturally, I wasn't a witness to Muriel's week, not close-up at least. As for Zachary, how I read it was that by Tuesday evening, his spirits and sense of self-worth, in terms of the investigation, had plummeted to a very low point. He began to let himself go physically, and a dark, pervasive sense of haplessness prevented him from gaining purchase on the slightest hope in the matter of Corrine. This, in part, was evidenced by the notes he recorded on March 13. These notes comprised more of a diary entry, as I discovered when I snooped around and read them later. Very little of the writing survived in his final report; evidently, he felt it contained too much subjectivity, or even self-pity.

March 11, 1995. Spent a second night at Johanna and Devon's house, but this time I requested it of them. I asked them outright if I could stay over. Privately, this freaks me out, that I did that. I was on their sofa again. I thought of Epilogue alone in the house, and it didn't set well. I told them right away that Muriel was in Durham at her university. I was quite aware that I risked having Muriel telephone and not find me home to all hours.

When I arrived, they were watching home movies. "The one we're watching now is of Corrine when she was four," Johanna said, "when we vacationed in Maine for a few days." I watched with them for the duration of that footage. Then Johanna set a place for me at the table, and served lamb meat loaf, mashed potatoes, cherry pie for dessert. "Cherries out of the can, I'm sorry to say." There wasn't much talking while we ate. When Devon cleared the dishes, he said, "We get maybe half of why you're here, Zachary—if we're on a first-name basis now. But I admit, the half we might understand may be just as perplexing as the half we don't. Do you want to enlighten us as to your motive for sleeping on our couch? When you have a nice home fifteen minutes away?" But I couldn't enlighten them. I just sat and ate a second piece of pie.

Johanna said, "To not talk's fine. Since Corrine went missing, everyone who comes into this house, they get all tongue-tied." I didn't want to—I couldn't bear to—foist any half-baked mystical thinking into the mix, like, "I just thought my being in this physical environment—the photographs of Corrine everywhere—might have some effect." Because I didn't subscribe to any extrasensory stuff at all, not at all. "Well, if anything comes to mind, let us know," Devon said. "We're going back into the den to watch more home movies. Which we'd like to do as a family, alone. You understand. As far as the bathroom and kitchen are concerned, make yourself at home." In fact, I woke up at 3 a.m., put a note on the kitchen table, and departed from the Moores' house. As I left, I noticed the yellow legal pad; it had some names, telephone numbers, and addresses crossed out, but many weren't.

It's so bleak out—I'm digressing here a little. Late November, say, all the bare trees and fields, on an overcast day it's like driving through a thousand different charcoal sketches or something like that. Then on into late March, spring's still a rumor, what with the hard-rutted back roads, passing by this or that farmhouse, say near Adamant—I'm over there a lot and have looked into many farmhouse windows there. I'm referring to the warmth of the interiors, which seems to almost make the cold seem colder. I wonder if Simon Inescort ever wrote about winters here. How would I know? I never read a word he wrote. Muriel's read two of his books, but neither in bed.

And clearly she's becoming real friends with his widow, Lorca Pell.

This. morning I had meetings at the agency. There's always ten or more pending cases. Some are the usual, jerks who violated parole, delinquent alimony payments, a young woman who bought a gun for some druggies near Burlington, and they used it to rob a bunch of general stores — they're in jail, our agency is looking for her. We're working with federal on that. A fellow who pried thousands of dollars' worth of barn boards off five different barns, stored the boards in a storage space on Route 2, and disappeared, possibly to up near Irasburg, where his son and ex-wife live. Oh, and there's a — and I wouldn't be caught dead using the word "favorite" at the office, but this one's secretly my favorite, just in terms of unusual human behavior, the kind of thing I can regale Muriel with, too — the woman who stole a donkey from a farm. She drove up to a barn late one night — nobody but the donkey was home — got the donkey up a ramp and into her pickup, and drove off. A phone repairman saw her drive west on Route 15, a mile or two out of Hardwick, and he told us when he dropped by our office, "I thought, That animal's going to jump out any minute now. Donkeys don't hide their anxieties — he's braying and kicking like crazy." It didn't stop there, either. Because this woman made postcards out of a photograph she had taken of herself with the donkey and mailed them out randomly — and I mean not necessarily to people she knew. She sent them all from the Johnson post office, though, the dimwit. The postmistress in Johnson gave a good description of a woman who purchased ten sheets of postcard stamps, so I'll follow up on that. Who hired us wasn't even the original owner of the donkey, though he's fuming. Who hired us was the donkey owner's sixty-three-year-old girl-friend — Muriel prefers to say "paramour" for older people — who'd given the donkey to the owner as a present this past Christmas. There's one of the perpetrator's postcards tacked to the bulletin board at work. In a meeting, Mr. Vlamick said, "Let's try and find out who took the photograph, all right? Or at least where it was developed, if possible." Mr. Vlamick offers a lot of homegrown wisdom about our profession, but I most prefer how Erica puts it: "A person can hide in Vermont as well as they can hide anywhere. Sooner or later — and there's been exceptions — they fuck up and are located."

At one p.m. I drove to St. Johnsbury on another lead. (I no longer say "promising lead.") But first I stopped in at Rainbow Sweets Bakery near the Marshfield Library. I ordered an empanada, a salad, and a ginger ale, with a coffee to go. Bill, the proprietor, was on the phone with his brother in Philadelphia. He had János Starker on his stereo system — I saw the CD case with Starker's picture on it; his expression was like his name, stark, but he played the cello like an angel. Bill's assistant, Emeline, prepared my lunch and served it. I'm only just getting to know Bill and his wife, Patricia, and I didn't expect him to drop everything to chat with me. He and Trish are great friends with Lorca, so we have that connection. He was friends with Simon, too. Muriel and I have had a couple of riotous Friday evenings in the bakery, when it was jammed with people, me and Muriel being sort of the new kids in town. Bill has a very seasoned sense of discretion about all things local; he knows I'm working the Corrine Moore case, but he doesn't ask. After paying my bill, I drove the twenty or so minutes to St. Johnsbury. There I spoke with a Mrs. Gail De Longhi, who'd left me a message at the agency. Her house was a big brick Victorian with a widow's walk atop the roof, located at 1374 Main Street, across from the Fairbanks Museum.

Mrs. De Longhi was an elegant-looking woman. Just a guess here, but I'd say she's about eighty. Immediately in the foyer I saw an array of family photographs, including three showing Mrs. De Longhi as a teenager, another in her late forties, and another when she was, let's say, around seventy. The words that came to mind were, What a stunning woman. Mrs. De Longhi gave no greeting, just turned around, and I followed her into her spacious living room.

"Set your coat anywhere," she said. She sat down in a rocking chair and drew a shawl around her shoulders. "Sit down there, Mr. Anders." She pointed to a sofa opposite her. "Or do you prefer *Detective* Anders?"

"Not necessary," I said. I set the tape recorder on the table between us and said, "Is this all right with you?"

She nodded yes. "I don't mind such formalities. In fact, formalities are a great comfort for me. I live alone. Besides a weekly housekeeper, I don't have help, and I prefer it that way."

The house was spacious and had magnificent chandeliers and a great rolltop writing desk. There was a small glass case displaying five quill pens.

Mrs. De Longhi had a few age spots on her forehead and hands. Her white hair was done up in two circular braids atop her head. She had on a dark red cotton blouse with a pattern of small birds, a black sweater, only the top button buttoned, and, a bit of a surprising contrast, fuddy-duddy bedroom slippers. She looked comfortable in her clothes. She wore earrings, a thin gold bracelet on her left wrist, a wedding ring, a string of pearls around her neck. Like I said, elegant. I'm listing all of this — formally — because my first impression was of a very poised, intelligent woman. In other words, not a nut case, to be crude about it, of the sort I'd been dealing with. But as Mr. Vlamick keeps warning me, you can't be swayed by appearances, you can be very wrong about appearances. I should be careful, in other words, not to automatically connect up Mrs. De Longhi's demeanor with the veracity of her sighting of Corrine Moore.

Impatient and tired, I was rudely thinking, Okay, I am happy to know all of this, it's very interesting, but can we please talk about your phone call now, please? Mrs. De Longhi then offered me tea, which I declined, and finally I said, "Mrs. De Longhi, the reason for your telephone call. Can you give me the details of what you saw?"

"Well, of course young man, I thought you'd never ask. You know, when a person listens so politely, he runs the risk of encouraging someone to talk. Before we get to the fact that I definitely saw Corrine Moore, poor child, let me speak on behalf of my clearness of mind, in the hopes of putting you at ease. You don't yet seem to be at ease. Turn around and look at the top shelf of books." I did as she asked and saw a complete set of red leather-bound books. "Those are the complete works of Arthur Conan Doyle," she said. "The Sherlock Holmes crime mysteries were the entirety of my husband's literary reading. He read medical books constantly, of course. And history. But I mention this because it's important for you to know that I've to this day not read a single Sherlock Holmes. Nor am I a local Miss Marple, and we have a few of those in town, believe me, busybodying all the time. Nor do I belong to a canasta or bridge club, quilting bee, or knitting circle, where old people sit around solving crimes by gossip, crimes that they've got from the newspaper. I read Jane Austen and George Eliot and Edith Wharton, and, when I got the okay from my heart doctor, some of Virginia Woolf. Cannot bear Henry James. Tried, but couldn't. All this is to say, Mr. Anders, dear investigator of one of the most uncivilized, heinous crimes imaginable, to take a little child like Corrine Moore from her family . . . This is to say, the old woman sitting in front of you has never taken life lightly, and I don't take this crime lightly, nor do I take lightly my responsibility here."

"I've got the tape recorder running, as you can see, Mrs. De Longhi."

"I shall be clear and deliberate," she said. "Two days ago, I used my ski poles to walk to the museum across the street. I generally arrive at eleven, have a cup of tea with whoever is overseeing the gift shop, or another staff member, even one of the Eye on the Sky meteorologists. I favor Steve Moleski, but confided in him once that sometimes, on the radio, it sounds like he is blaming Canada for everything.

"That morning, I noticed a school bus parked out front. An hour later, once I'd had tea with Evelyn Simic, who is part-time in the gift shop, I was quite prepared to return home and work out a recipe for my dinner. That's when I heard some commotion coming from the main display room, where the taxidermied bears and other mammals reside, and various dioramas and glass cases full of insects pinned to cushions. A gaggle of children—I'd have to guess third- or fourth-graders—were coming up from the planetarium, all chatter and restlessness, as you'd expect. Here they'd been looking at the vast universe, but apparently had nonetheless felt confined. Oh, well. So, here they came, and for some reason I was drawn to this. This, which I'd seen hundreds of times, school groups traipsing through halls and exhibits. But then there was a small cacophony. It consisted mostly of laughter, but add a little alarm. Some children were pointing. Not a teacher or parent chaperone in sight, if you can imagine such a thing.

"I suppose some old docent instinct flared up in me, and I walked right over, quite prepared to dish out a reprimand. But when I arrived to the polar bear, reared up on its hind legs, lo and behold, standing inside the stanchion right next to the bear was a little girl. She was dressed in her winter coat, with a stocking cap which didn't at all hide her face, and she had on rain galoshes—rather strange, considering the snow. Surrounded by all those children, she suddenly flew into a panic and ran out the museum's front door.

"This brings me to the reason I telephoned your office, Mr. Anders. The reason I telephoned within a half hour of the incident, if I may call it that. This is why I telephoned with such urgency. Coincidence, or fate, or whatnot, or luck—while the aforementioned commotion was taking place, Evelyn Simic was doing something she shouldn't, as a responsible employee of the museum, have been doing. You see, the gift shop carried small plastic cameras in pastel colors, a novelty item. Decaled on the camera were the faces of famous artists, like Picasso and Leonardo. That morning, Evelyn, I don't know what put larceny into her—"

Mrs. De Longhi reached into a cloth shopping bag and

took out and handed me one of the cameras she was telling me about. It was pastel green, with a decal of Toulouse-Lautrec. My heart nearly stopped, as if it registered a little ahead of my brain where her story was heading. I got myself together and said, "Mrs. De Longhi, are you about to tell me that Evelyn took a picture of Corrine Moore?"

"I was about to, if you'd stop interrupting," she said. "Now, having looked at the photographs on the poster, and those in the newspaper, and on the evening news, I can now say for certain: it was Corrine Moore who stood next to the polar bear. Now, for the life of me I cannot account for what gift of intuition Evelyn gave to the situation when she snapped a picture of Corrine. Yes, she snapped a picture, all right. But whether or not it caught Corrine fully enough to identify her, that I cannot say."

"This very camera I'm holding?" I asked.

"I took up a collection from my own purse and paid for it outright to Evelyn," she said, "because I wanted to own it until I gave it to you, or to the police. Then I carried it back home. And now you have it, Mr. Anders."

"I'm wondering, middle of the day and all by herself . . . Where were her abductors, I wonder."

"I told you, I've never read Sherlock Holmes."

"Just thinking out loud, sorry," I said.

"Do you know something? Every day for the last decade, I've taken a nap right about now."

I stood up to go and said, "I'll be in touch as soon as I get this film developed. Thank you. I can't thank you enough."

Then Mrs. De Longhi said, "Before you leave, there's one more thing to mention. There's one more thing to give to you. Do you know, Mr. Anders, what those children were pointing at? Yes, of course, it was the little girl inside the stanchion. But when she ran out of the museum, look what I found fastened to the bear, with a clothespin, of all things." She again reached into her cloth bag and handed me one of the MISSING CHILD posters with Corrine's picture on it. "Don't you think this points to the fact that Corrine knows she's missing?"

I thanked Mrs. De Longhi again. I got a little too worked up and actually kissed her hand. I'd never mention that at the agency.

The office was closed, so I drove directly to Erica's house. Her car wasn't in the driveway, but Erica often parked it in her garage. I looked up the road and saw the lights on in our farmhouse, but of course Muriel was in Durham. I honked the horn, then got out of my truck, hurried up her stone steps, and pounded on the door, then opened it a little and shouted, "Erica! It's Zachary — you home?" But there was no response. I walked right in and left a note — *Call me! Zachary.* I drove up the road and parked across from our farmhouse. Inside, I called and left a message on Mr. Vlamick's home telephone; once he heard it, I knew he'd call me no matter what time it was. I was very detailed in what I said. I then tried to reach Muriel. No luck there, either.

I can take it from there. At about eight o'clock, Zachary made a peanut butter and jelly sandwich. Every ten or fifteen minutes for the next two hours, he dialed Muriel's number. Then Erica showed up. She did exactly what Zachary had done at her house, which was to knock loudly, open the door, and shout, "Zachary — you home?"

Zachary heard something from his office, went into the guest room, looked out the window, saw Erica's car, lifted the storm window, and yelled down, "Erica, come in!"

Erica hurried straight up the stairs and into Zachary's office. Breathlessly, she said, "Zachary, you won't believe what I found out." She didn't bother to take her coat off, but started right in: "The orchids—from your report. The orchids were really bothering me."

The plastic camera was right on the desk. "How do you mean?" Zachary asked.

"In your report, you talked about taking orchid petals to what's-her-face, the florist?"

"Kelly Shrift."

"Right, and so you wrote that she identified the orchid as whatsit?"

"Lovely Lavender Orchid."

"I hate lavender," Erica said. "But anyway, let me get out my notes. Okay, let me find . . . Okay, listen. So like I said, the orchid stuff was nagging at me and nagging at me. Then I remembered from your report what Devon Moore said about his greenhouse assistants."

"Frances and Robert Tremain. I spoke with them for a few minutes at the greenhouse. I have notes around here somewhere."

"Well, this morning I talked with them for over an hour. I tried to reach you, to tell you I was going to do this, but I couldn't fucking reach you, Zach."

"Tell me."

"What I'm saying is, the orchid thing bothered me. The

orchid thing. The orchid thing. Then I remembered this
married couple you mentioned — just a sentence or two,
right? In your report. How they worked for Devon Moore
in his greenhouse, right? So I read your report again. It was
two things that made me decide to interview them. First,
you wrote down that Devon called them 'quick studies.'
And second, you wrote — it's right here in my notes — you
wrote Devon said, 'They have a bickering relationship with
the world.' These two things grated together, were like —
like what? Like fingernails on a blackboard in my brain. It
kept irking me, I was fucking irked, Zachary, and I tried to
reach you. I called up their house in St. J. Robert Tremain
answers, I properly identify myself, I used the words 'routine follow-up conversation,' all like that, and I asked if I can
drive over to speak with them, I'd just be a few minutes, I
said. And here's a third irksome thing. He said, 'Oh, don't
bother, we'll meet you somewhere. Where would you like
to meet?' I mean, it couldn't have been clearer: they didn't
want me anywhere near their house. One hour and fifteen
minutes later, I'm sitting across from them in a booth at the
Wayside. I get the French dip sandwich, they both just get
coffee, which I get, too. I am taking a bite like every five minutes, because coffee alone would go way too fast to allow any
substance in the conversation, right?"

"I hope to God you had your tape recorder on."

"Crotch of my jeans, the zipper open for better reception.
I tried not to move too much down there, and we can listen
later — I've already listened. You'll hear most of it loud and
clear, take my word for it. I am so good at this shit, Zachary,

and the only reason I'm so good at it, this getting at things roundabout, by indirection, odd slants, and I got so good at it because I fucked it up so many times early on in my career, I had to get better. Like I said, we can listen to it later—or right now if you want. But the interview gave me the creeps. The creeps, Zachary. Oh, they answered all my questions in a perfectly reasonable manner. It wasn't that. It was, in the end, something the creep Frances said. She said, in a creepy, confiding way like we were bonding, she says, 'We're getting sick of orchids. In fact, we're looking for other work closer to home, in St. J.'

"Then I drove straight over to the Moores' house. As you know, I already knew them, so I acted like it was a casual drop-by, just checking in, reiterating that I was working with you, et cetera. And while we were having a coffee, I said, like out of the blue but of course not out of the blue, I said, 'My partner Zachary said you were having some show-up-to-work discontinuity problems with your greenhouse workers—how's that working out?' And I've got to tell you, without a moment's hesitation, Devon got his hackles up and he says, 'This isn't a matter for you, professionally, but as if things couldn't get even worse—' And Johanna cuts right in and says, 'Devon thinks they're stealing orchids. He keeps pretty close tabs.' I acted totally nonchalant and said, 'Well, for a later time, maybe. I hope it isn't true, but it's not of much importance in the bigger picture, right?' But it *was* the bigger picture, Zachary. It *is* part of the bigger picture, my friend. It is a matter for us, *professionally.* You're fucking-A right it is."

"This is incredible, Erica," Zachary said. "Because me, too,

I've got a tape for you to listen to, and you really have to listen to it now."

"I'm all ears — in a minute," Erica said. "Because there's one last thing, a thing the creep Robert Tremain said. He didn't say much at the Wayside, but he said enough. He says — I was asking how they spent their free time, you know, when they weren't working at the greenhouse. And Tremain says, 'Well, you see, we're childless, and so we go for drives a lot, and we have our TV programs, and —' And right then and there I think, Why in the fuck did he use the word 'childless'? Zachary, I think these two creeps took Corrine Moore."

Zachary looked stunned. "Erica, please listen to my tape," he said. "Just sit here with me and listen to it. Then, see this little plastic camera?" Zachary held up the camera. "We have to get the film in it developed — now. Tonight. You have to tell me how and where. It has to be developed on an emergency basis."

"Turn the thing on. Who are you interviewing?"

"A Mrs. De Longhi, in her house in St. Johnsbury."

"As in the wife of Dr. De Longhi, now deceased? Who got the Governor's Award for good deeds? The De Longhi Medical Center's named after him. Where is it? Williston?"

"Has to be one and the same."

I played Erica the tape. The only thing she said afterward was "I'm hyperventilating. I need a glass of water."

Erica placed the camera in her handbag and said, "We're going to the police forensic lab in Waterbury. It's less than an hour. First I'm going to use your phone and call Sharon Allen. She's a crack photography expert who works there, she's the very best, and at this time of night she'll be home, which is Burlington. We're friends since the stone age, and she'll get right in her car."

"Use the phone in our bedroom."

She went into the bedroom, took her wallet out of her handbag, went through half a dozen cards, found the one she was looking for, set the wallet on the bedside table, and made the call.

Back in Zachary's office, she said, "Sharon's en route. When we get to Waterbury, we have to call the BCI. We have to call the DPS. State police, we have to call. We have to wake everyone up if need be. Jesus H. Christ, Zachary, Corrine Moore is locatable!"

Zachary set the alarm code and they were out the door.

MURIEL STEPPED INTO THE FARMHOUSE at 11:30 p.m., a day earlier than originally planned. She went upstairs, calling "Eppy, Eppy, Eppy." Throwing herself onto the bed, exhausted, she saw the wallet. She picked it up, opened it, and saw that the driver's license belonged to Erica. "That's weird," she said. Epilogue jumped up on the bed, making his usual seismic appearance. "Hey, Eppy, come here, my perfect boy." Epilogue pushed up against Muriel's leg and she stroked under his chin and scratched behind his ears. Then she telephoned Erica's number. I could hear Erica's voicemail answer. "Erica, it's Muriel Streuth," Muriel said. "You left your wallet here. In the bedroom, oddly enough. Sorry to call so late. I'll put it on the kitchen counter."

Downstairs, Muriel took out a bottle of whiskey from

the pantry, poured a shot, and threw it back, then sat in the living room and sorted through her mail, taken from the wicker basket in the kitchen. Epilogue joined her on the sofa. "Look at that, will you, Eppy?" Muriel said. "The fire's not died down, but no husband in sight. And now that we have this private moment, I need to say, I think it's you causing the alarm to go off. I don't know how. I may never know how. But lately I'm beginning to suspect you. I'm not saying you're doing it on purpose, either."

She went into the bathroom and drew a hot bath. The door was open, and when I saw her clothes strewn on the floor, I went and sat in the library. Muriel stayed in the tub a good two hours, replenishing the hot water at necessary intervals; I heard the spigot, which was a touch rusty. Beethoven string quartets had ended. But what then occurred entirely distracted me from the pages of the grim *Mayor of Casterbridge.* I heard Muriel singing. She could barely hold a tune, but was nonetheless belting out the schmaltzy torch song "My Funny Valentine," and it was delightful to hear she knew it by heart. When she croakily stretched out the word *val-en-tiiine,* she fell into racking sobs. She didn't cry for very long. For all of my previous lack of inhibition, if that's what to call it, in chronicling just about everything in the farmhouse, somehow hearing this made me feel I should be elsewhere. Yet my armchair psychologist's guess was that to some degree Muriel felt a surge of remorse about Valentine's Day. But that has to be too simple, doesn't it? That was my one thought, though I felt, in her cracking voice, and in the silence that followed, deeper complexities of feeling.

From the bathtub at around 2 a.m., Muriel must have

seen the glow of headlights through the bathroom window. She got out of the bath. Wearing a robe and slippers, holding the robe's collar tightly closed at the neck, she went into the kitchen. When Zachary and Erica walked in, Zachary said, "I saw your car! I called and called and couldn't reach you." Zachary threw off his coat, kissed and embraced Muriel, and said, "I'm over the moon you're back, sweetheart. We have big news."

Over Zachary's shoulder, Muriel said, "Where were you so late, Erica?"

"Long, long night," Erica said. "I'll just get my wallet here, thanks, and then Zachary can fill you in."

Erica was out the door. Zachary stepped back and said, "I didn't expect to see you till tomorrow, earliest. I tried to reach you. Everything go okay at school?"

"But you're happy to see me, right here and now, right?"

"Like I said, over the moon. How can you ask me that?"

"What was Erica's wallet doing in our bedroom?"

"She left it there."

"When?"

"Let's sit down." He took Muriel by the hand and led her into the living room. They sat on the sofa. "Erica came over, I don't know what time. The thing was, I desperately needed to talk with her."

"Because?"

"Because, there's about to be an arrest."

"God in heaven. When?"

"This morning, I'd say by seven a.m., maybe earlier. I intend to be there. Erica does, too. Various law enforcement people are going to the house of Robert and Frances Tremain, residents of St. Johnsbury."

"They kidnapped Corrine?"

"Everything points to them."

"But where were you with Erica?"

"It's a long story, and I'm going to tell it to you in detail till your ears drop off. But for starters, me and Erica had to go to the forensic lab in Waterbury, because, guess what? A woman working in the gift shop at the Fairbanks Museum snapped a photograph of Corrine Moore. And less than two hours ago, me and Erica saw this photograph, right from the darkroom. It's definitely Corrine. And, I don't want to jinx it, but unless something too terrible to think about's happened to her over the last two days, Corrine Moore is very much alive."

"Life will change for all good people now, right?"

"I tried to reach you, Murr."

"I had some sort of bug, not quite the flu, I don't think. Work was practically nonstop, a lot of hand-holding. Plus which, Kazumi had a personal setback, and I was her shrink for what felt like twenty-four hours straight. But that's all for later, Zach. For later later later . . ."

"No way will I be able to sleep. I'll wait for a call and then jump in the pickup and drive straight to St. Johnsbury."

"I'll stay up with you, of course."

"You've had a bath, I see."

"There's plenty of hot water left."

"I think we should go upstairs."

Zachary showered quickly. Once under the bedclothes, they held each other and both seemed almost hypnotized

by the fire through the glass window of the woodstove.
"We've been in different places, haven't we, a little," Zachary said.

"Yes, I think so. A little. Just across the river waving to
each other, maybe."

"There's been reasons."

They didn't speak for a while. "Want me to recite?" Muriel finally said. "My very favorite of the Korin poems — my
translations got final approval from the vixens. Well, Kazumi never really gives full approval, but so be it. It's all for
the best, because once I realized she was impossible to please,
I could please myself with the work I was doing. Anyway,
here goes:

You say there's no self, then who tells you
what words you speak in your sleep?
You say there's no self, then who is it
makes you laugh each time I scatter
the mandarin ducks over the wet grass?
You say there's no self, then who is it
you so painfully miss each time I row away
in moonlight?

"Now comes the part inside parentheses, Zach," Muriel
said.

(Sure, there's the famous "Thirty-Six Views of——" but no one knows of
"One View of My Great Love, Unclothed, One Hand Between Her
Legs, the Other Stirring the Water of Her Bath")

"End parentheses," Muriel said. Then she read the rest of the poem:

Strengthless to rise from the pond,
a dragonfly still desires sun on its wings.
Strengthless to rise from candle wax,
a moth still unfolds its two hand-painted fans.
Strengthless to lift her head from a school desk,
the young student sleeps
until she is one hundred.

"Muriel," Zachary said, "before you left for Durham, you said you needed to do some serious thinking. I thought you meant about school stuff. A lecture you had to give, maybe. But later I wasn't so sure."

Muriel moved a little apart, propped herself up against the pillows. Zachary didn't like the distance. He leaned over, took the nipple of Muriel's right breast in his mouth for a brief moment; she held his head in her hands. They had a long kiss. Muriel then held out her hands, a kind of Diana Ross stop-in-the-name-of-love choreographic gesture, and said, "I don't mind talking all night, my darling, but if we are talking, we should probably just talk."

"Pull the blanket up, then."

But Muriel did the opposite. She flung the blanket aside, rolled over onto her stomach, and looked back in the half-light of the woodstove, posing like an Ingres odalisque.

"That will make talking harder," Zachary said.

"If talk is what's getting hard, then I'll go make tea."

Muriel turned, embraced Zachary, and said, "I promise to tell you my deepest thoughts later."

I went downstairs to the library and picked up *The Mayor of Casterbridge* again, page after page of Hardy's bleak moors and blazing fireplaces unable to warm the hearts of his loneliest bachelors and widows, all providing such a heart-wrenching contrast to what ensued upstairs in the farmhouse.

After I'd read forty or so pages, Epilogue suddenly leapt from the typewriter and, for no discernible reason, began to act like he was inside a pinball machine, bouncing from bookshelf to bookshelf, off the chair, off the window that faced the barn. Then the MOTION IN LIBRARY alarm went off. I heard a burst of Muriel's laughter and then the sound of her stomping down the stairs, saying, "Shut up! Shut up! Shut up!" And when she hurried past the library, I saw she had on just a flannel shirt. Her hands were clamped over her ears. Epilogue was now crouched under the library desk, hissing in my direction.

Muriel went into the kitchen. "That's it. I've had it." Predictably, the telephone rang, and when Muriel picked up, she said, "This is Muriel Streuth. Everything's fine. I'm here with my husband. It's all fine. But it's the same as last time — you can check your computer records — the alarm was not set, but still it went off. I'll call you tomorrow about this." She hung up.

I took *The Collected Poems of Wallace Stevens* from the shelf and set it on the floor directly over the sensor under the rug. When Muriel walked into the library, she saw the book, picked it up, started jumping up and down, then whirled in a circle, waving it in the air (I realized at that moment that

I'd done what I'd sworn never to do, which was intervene),
shouting, "Get out! Get out! Get out!" until she got so worn
out, she threw herself onto the library's sofa.

Zachary called downstairs, "What's going on?"

"I'm chasing Wallace Stevens out of our library," Muriel
shouted. "He's been setting off the alarm all along!" In the
kitchen, Muriel put on coffee, and in a few minutes she set
her and Zachary's steaming cups on the table in front of the
woodstove. She added two logs to the fire. Dressed in his
robe and T-shirt, Zachary came down and sat on the sofa.

"Kazumi's got this ambitious idea of translating the poems
of Wallace Stevens into Japanese," Muriel said. "I'm going to
give her my copy of his poems. I think it might solve our
alarm problem."

"I'll trust you in this," Zachary said.

It was after three in the morning. They looked out at the
falling snow, which seemed to emanate its own light. "I like
our life a whole lot just now," Muriel said.

Nothing said, nothing said. Then: "This might surprise
you a little," Muriel said, "but I've got to credit, of all people, Ardith Paleo here. For providing me some perspective
on our life, yours and mine. This last Monday night, down in
Portsmouth, we all had a kind of slumber party at Kazumi's
house. I wasn't feeling all that great — sniff sniff sniff and a
slight sore throat. But we had a fun time. Lots of shop talk.

"There'd been a sleet storm, phones were out for a while,
electricity. Kazumi's got a gas stove, so we made pasta. It got
late, and suddenly I detected some tension, and I found out
later, during Kazumi's confession and pity-poor-me session,
that she and Ardith were having certain *conflicts*. Well, it's still

early days, maybe, but there's a very strong thing going on with them, I am rooting for them, love is hard to find. But Monday night, before the tension, and this was said in a sincere way, Zach. Ardith began to talk about all the pressure you must be under, with the investigation, with Corrine Moore. They knew a little about it, but I hadn't gone into much detail. But, you know, the pressures. What with us being so new to the community. 'You've got your own anxieties, too,' she said to me. 'Getting your book handed in, all the end-of-semester crap. But let's face it, academic problems are mostly luxurious problems, not life and death.' So, sweetheart, there was this very edgy, very brilliant, very opinionated woman. Offering perspective. At one point, she paged through a notebook and launched into a sort of mini-lecture about something Mencius said."

"Is he an academic colleague of yours?"

"After Confucius, the most revered ancient Chinese philosopher. As it turns out, David, the fellow who constructed the stone wall for the little cemetery Simon Inescort's buried in? He actually translated a whole volume of Mencius."

"Interesting road we live on. Though I think we need another private investigator, to balance out the literary types."

"The thing is, Mencius is important to some of the essays Ardith is writing. Me, personally, I'm at best an ignoramus when it comes to Chinese philosophy, so I was all ears. Ardith's *perspective*—as it pertained to our marriage. But mostly how it pertained to your trying so hard to find Corrine Moore."

"And what was her perspective?"

"I didn't exactly memorize it, Zach. But the heart of it

was, and this comes from Mencius. I'm quoting: The most grounded work for the sake of a community is the rescue of an abandoned child. To rescue an abandoned or lost child is proof of our humanity."

"That's a little over my head."

"I doubt it. Whatever, it's not above what you and Erica actually accomplished, though."

They sipped coffee awhile. Epilogue sauntered in and stretched out in front of the woodstove. He yawned. He rose up and walked to his water dish, lapped up water, returned to the woodstove. He sat there staring at Muriel. He closed his eyes. Muriel and Zachary both looked at their cat.

"Well, I need to tell you, we're soon going to need perspective on something else," Muriel said. "Like in the next thirty seconds."

She pulled Zachary close and placed his hand flat on her belly. "At the clinic on campus I found out I'm *with child*."

Zachary stood up. He sat down. He kissed Muriel's belly, and then they had a lingering kiss on the lips, and she said, "I accept the order those kisses came in. It's what's-its-name's first kiss from Dad. I think we shouldn't tell anyone for three months, to play it safe, Zach, you know? I asked at the clinic. But no harm in discussing names. I made a list in my head driving home."

"Why didn't you tell me right away?"

"Things needed to settle down. Think about it. Between news of Corrine—and you have to go any minute to St. Johnsbury. Those hideous kidnappers, they won't have guns, will they?"

"I'll be there with every cop in the state."

"Talk about perspective. It's like two children have been found on the same night. The Moores' news. Our news."

"Speaking of our news, those Japanese poems must've worked wonders."

"It had to be the quality of my translations."

"Had to be."

"Zachary, things should be stated directly in a marriage, right?"

"Always, except when it's best not to."

"A book I found right after I was at the clinic, it says that pregnancy can make things quite steamy in bed. In case you're worried."

"I'm not. But where'd you find this book? I think I should read it."

"I found it at the Portsmouth Public Library. You should see how often it was checked out. The due date card was stamped even in the margins."

Hearing Muriel's and Zachary's news, I was overwhelmed with happiness, and yet, inevitably, I again felt so sad for Lorca and me. How to rise above? I remembered a Jewish proverb about how life should always take precedence: When a wedding meets a funeral on the road, the funeral should step aside.

Zachary got the call at 4:45 a.m., and he was out the door by 5:00.

THE
GHOST
CLAUSE

TODAY, WITHIN THE ONGOINGNESS, a memory arrived
unbidden, as memories always do. I had been sitting in
the library, reading Wallace Stevens, when I looked up and
noticed that Muriel had added something new to the library
wall: the framed copy of the original deed, which contained
the ghost clause.

I had long thought that, in one way or another, almost
every day Lorca and I spent in the house connected us to
the past. The architecture itself; the columned chronicle
of the heights of children formerly in residence, written in
pencil alongside the pantry door; the decays and repairs; the
vague smell of lightning that never leaves the nearest maple and drifts in through the library's screened window on
the breeze; moss on the roof shingles; secret passageways of
mice; the morning, midday, and evening light striking each
window differently; a century's layers of white paint, maybe
more than a century's; the branch that, after decades, finally reaches a length where a squirrel can acrobat onto the
roof; wallpaper that peels away to reveal other wallpaper;

the discarded rectangles of gravestones that some previous owner used to shore up and balance the back porch; the hieroglyphic porcupine toothmarks on the stanchions under the mudroom; how the bases of bedposts made barely detectable indentations in the planks, through generations of lovemaking and when children hopped on beds like trampolines.

Every nook and cranny archives time. Built in 1845, sure, yet who knows, maybe for the farmhouse these are still early days. I've thought of the house as "here before the Civil War," perhaps because I like to think of it first existing at a relatively peaceful time in Vermont. Lorca and I learned that for five years it served as a music school. There were no classrooms per se, but various instructors of piano, violin, viola, flute, even harpsicord and harp, would be paid a small fee to teach students in the downstairs rooms. If the teachers arrived from long distances, they stayed over in the upstairs bedrooms. We read in a diary written by a neighbor from that period that a violin and a woodwind teacher had fallen in love in the farmhouse, each having traveled from upstate New York, a long way back then, for employment. I once attempted (I fell short) to write a novel based on their courtship. Once, when Lorca had pneumonia and had spiked a fever of 104, she claimed that, tossing and turning in sweaty sheets one night in our bed, she heard harpsicord music floating in the air.

And then, three months after I died, I observed a widow in her privacy, which you don't often see except in certain classical paintings. I was standing out front of the farmhouse, looking in through the library window, and there was Lorca, sitting in the rocking chair, reading *Middlemarch*. I cannot tell you how many times she went on George Eliot jags, and one year she read not only three George Eliot novels, but a collection of essays, too. At least once a year she read *Middlemarch,* but readily admitted that, when picking up the novel to read again, she didn't always start on page 1. She called that reading *in Middlemarch*.

Then Lorca set the book down on the rocker, sat at her desk, and looked to be writing out a list of some sort. Later, when I looked, I saw she had jotted down notes—1, 2, 3, 4, 5—of things to be sure to tell prospective buyers when she toured them through our house. It gave me a start, but then again, I wasn't totally surprised. Well, I was and I wasn't, that she had decided to sell. In the end, she refused to work with a realtor. She just sent word out, mainly through Vanessa at the co-op, and it made me smile to remember what Lorca had said about her: "If you want something known, tell the BBC or tell Vanessa."

One evening, I followed Lorca through the house as she rehearsed a tour. She auditioned tones of voice, separated out certain details from things we'd read in the historical society bulletins, but mostly chose anecdotes from her own experiences. Her voice broke during her description of the enormous wood-burning stove, and that the library was once the birthing room. Yet as it turned out, only one tour was necessary. Realtors call making a house presentable for strangers "staging," but Lorca wasn't about to do that. When speaking of our house to friends or acquaintances, she often called it *haimish,* a Yiddish word meaning something like "cozy and lived in." That is clearly how she wanted to present our house.

It was our cartoonist friend Ed, within a day or two of word getting out that Lorca intended to sell, who had suggested Muriel and Zachary. On the phone with Lorca—she had the speakerphone on while she continued to make a pasta sauce—he vouched for them. "Muriel Streuth and Zachary Anders," he said. "Different last names for professional reasons—she's a professor in New Hampshire, he's an investigator, has a new job with an agency in Montpelier—but they're definitely married."

"I've jotted down their names," Lorca said.

"I'd say they're a solid couple. They carry themselves well. They've been renting here in Brookfield, but they want to find their own place."

"Ed, of course they come highly recommended, because it's dear old you telling me about them."

"How are you, Lorca?"

"Oh, big question full of little daily things that seem to add up to, I'm just okay, I suppose. The moment I heard your voice, I wanted to say, 'Simon and you were such dear friends.'"

"I miss him a lot. We had our boys' nights out."

"Conversations as secret lives, Simon called it."

"I don't quite know how to say this. But are you sure you want to sell the house?"

"It's too much for me."

"I understand."

"Too much on so many levels, in so many ways, Ed. But we all had such great times here, didn't we?"

"Yes we did. When can you drive down for dinner?"

"I don't feel I'd be very good company."

"You can't seriously think that would matter to us."

"In a week or so, then."

"Do you know where you'll live?"

"I'm going to move into the apartment above the Adamant co-op. My studio's already there, as you know. There's three big rooms, and I've got carpenters lined up. They just need a start date. To add a good-sized bathroom, quite luxurious. Claw-foot tub and all of that."

"Your atelier in Adamant, Vermont."

"I'll be considered the expat from East Calais."

"That's actually pretty funny."

"You asked how I was doing. Not so good some days, less good others."

"Me and Curtis will drive up or meet you in town. Or you come here, okay?"

"The drawing you made, and what you said at the memorial, meant the world to me. I'm having the drawing framed."

"I'll have this young couple get in touch."

"Look, why not ask them to come over this Sunday? Give them directions to the house, will you?"

"Bye-bye. See you soon."

That Sunday morning at eleven o'clock, a Toyota pickup with Vermont plates pulled up across from the house. Muriel was at the wheel. She parked next to Lorca's 1985 Volvo wagon—my pickup was in the barn—which had over 200,000 miles on it and ran like a Swiss watch. I stood looking out the front living room window, open to its screen. It had been a seasonably warm early September, but this day, under a clear blue sky, had a slight chill in the air; you could hear rain in the trees from the previous night's storm.

Muriel was wearing blue jeans, a yellow cotton sweater, black flats. She had a veritable cascade of hair, perhaps a shade lighter auburn than Lorca's, and it looked to me, by the expression on her face as she took in the farmhouse, that she was already convinced. But it's possible that I may have conflated her expression with Lorca's when she herself had first seen the house. Memory intervenes, memory confuses, right? Zachary was about half an inch taller than Muriel. He held a notebook and pen. A man who wanted to check his observations later, I thought. He wore neatly pressed khaki trousers, a black T-shirt under a blue cotton work shirt, also neatly ironed. Looking at the farmhouse roof, he jotted something down.

After formal introductions were made in the kitchen, Lorca offered coffee and homemade lemon squares, but only Muriel accepted. She carried her cup of coffee and ate a lemon square while on Lorca's tour.

"We can go out to the barn later, if you want," Lorca said. "It's a sight to see."

Lorca commenced with a somewhat hesitant tone, but fairly soon she changed to a conversational one. She told how the house was built in 1845, and how the eldest two of the Peck family sons fought in the Civil War and had survived. She showed them a photograph of a Peck family reunion, at a long table set in front of the house. "The pantry has such low counters," Lorca said, "because Will Peck's wife, Dorothy, was quite a short woman." They toured the dining room and living room, and Lorca pointed out their wide ceiling beams. Then they walked into the library. "You're a literary scholar, or professor, isn't that right, Muriel?"

"So far I'm just an adjunct professor," Muriel said.

"I'm thinking you might like this library."

Lorca talked about the family photographs, in frames in the front hallway. Then her tour proceeded upstairs. "As you can see, the master bedroom has the sweeping view. It's a room with five doors, too. If you crane your neck a little, you can look out and just see the roof of my husband's cabin. He wrote some of his books up there. Some summers he practically lived up there, it seemed."

After Lorca revealed all the storage spaces, everyone went downstairs and into the kitchen, where Lorca asked Muriel and Zachary to sit with her at the table. There she spoke about the artesian well. About the neighbors. About the acreage and property tax. About the oil furnace and woodstoves. "If you're not comfortable with woodstoves, you might consider propane," Lorca said. "Woodstoves are demanding. But they're so comfy middle of winter, you know."

"It's a wonderful house," Muriel said.

"I should tell you something right away," Lorca said. "I won't expect you to be comfortable with it, either. But if you go up to the cabin, you'll see this lovely little cemetery. It's got a stone wall, built by our neighbor. Anyway, there's just the one gravestone so far. My husband Simon's. But I'd like to be buried there, too. I went through all the legal petitions and paperwork with the town clerk and the state, and so now there lies my husband. That's the thing — I intend to visit him as often as I like, as you might expect. Of course, if you'd like me to call ahead of time, while I'd prefer not to, I would. So you see, no matter what you might use the cabin for eventually, the little cemetery must stay as is. I'll be fully responsible for its upkeep."

Muriel waited a moment, then said, "You would never need to call ahead. Isn't that right, Zachary?"

"Mrs. Inescort, of course," Zachary said. "I noticed some interesting trees up there."

"My husband planted Japanese crabapples."

"The climate obviously suits them."

"I might have some more planted. Simon had an orchard in mind."

Lorca made Muriel a second cup of coffee.

"It's a really wonderful house," Zachary said.

Lorca looked out to the field in back. For a moment, I thought, perhaps because of the word "wonderful," that she might be having second thoughts. We had heard of that phenomenon, someone suddenly changing their mind about selling, even as late as when the deed was about to be transferred, the bill of sale about to be signed, all parties present and accounted for. And so now I half expected Lorca to say, "I'll be in touch," or something along those lines.

"Lorca, it has to be so difficult, even thinking about leaving here," Muriel said. "So much life obviously lived. So much life."

"You know, I'm pretty good at accessing a foretaste of regret, you might say," Lorca said. "Knowing ahead of time if I'd desperately regret something. I admit to some sleepless nights over selling the house. Over this decision. But it's right for me, at this point in life."

Silence for a few minutes. "Here's something else," Lorca finally said. "Some time ago, we discovered there was something called a ghost clause written into the original deed, back in the day. It was the deed that Will Peck's widow signed over to the next owner, a man named Harold Teachout. He owned the Inn at Long Last, south of here, in Chester. But he wanted to sell it and move here. The crux of the ghost clause is, if the seller of the house is aware of a malevolent . . . *entity* occupying the house, the seller has to inform the purchaser of it ahead of time. Because if it turns out this entity is a rabble-rouser of some sort—or I suppose however 'malevolent' might be interpreted—then the seller is obligated to repurchase the house. Say, for instance, I knew there was a malevolent ghost, and it threw pots and pans around or something—anything. I'd have to buy back the house from you, no questions asked. The validity of reporting such things is unassailable, and I mean in a court of law. And I guess that'd still hold up, too."

"Did you and your husband ever . . . ?" Zachary said.

"Oh, goodness, no," Lorca said. She was shaking her head slowly back and forth. "Goodness, goodness, no. No malevolent spirit did we ever experience. Ever."

"Well, how about a benevolent one?" Zachary asked.

"Not that, either," Lorca said. "Not on these premises. I mean, this is an old farmhouse. It's got its creak-creaks, a warp in some post or other, whatnot. It readily offers its complaints, that's for sure. But when my husband was alive, I did that, too."

They all fell into genuine laughter. Muriel actually spit out some coffee, which made everyone laugh more.

"Tell me more of who you both are," Lorca said. "That would help."

Muriel mentioned her doctoral work at Tufts University, and that she was going to defend her dissertation in December. "I'm confident it'll turn into something more full-time," she said. "I've been encouraged to have that confidence by the department chair."

"She's turning her dissertation into a book," Zachary said. "She's got a university press more than interested."

"That's impressive," Lorca said.

Muriel looked uncomfortable at having boasted even the little she had, but still, she had spoken truthfully.

"And you, Zachary?" Lorca asked.

"Well, I'm the new guy, junior investigator at the Green Mountain Agency in Montpelier. Though I did have experience with an agency in Saratoga Springs. But Muriel and I want to live in Vermont. Even though it's a commute for her."

"You may not realize it, but just next door is Erica Heilman, an investigator herself," Lorca said. "An estimable one."

"Great reputation," Zachary said. "I've talked with her a few times on the phone. I never knew where she lived, though."

"Next house down."

"That'd make—I mean—" Zachary said.

"If things should work out," Muriel said.

"Yes," said Lorca, "that would mean two investigators on the same road."

"By my lights, the Green Mountain Agency is fortunate to have Zachary," Muriel said. "They must feel the same, because they've assigned him a very urgent, very . . . I don't know what. *Devastating* case."

"Oh, yes, and what case is that, if I may ask?" Lorca said. "If you're allowed to talk about it."

"It's public knowledge," Zachary said. "I'm lead in a missing child case."

"I take it you mean Corrine Moore," Lorca said. "I've known Corrine since she was born."

"I'm sorry to even mention it," Zachary said. "It's got to be hard on everyone in this community."

"For Johanna and Devon, a waking nightmare," Lorca said. "I have a painting studio over the Adamant co-op, not a half mile from the Moores' house."

"So far, I'm solely assigned," Zachary said. "There's been complaints about that, because I'm new. But I worked on a missing child case—a little boy—in New York State, right near Saratoga Springs, in fact. What that turned out to be, a father took off with his son, acrimonious marriage situation. So, Green Mountain saw that I had a specific kind of experience."

"My husband's a very ethical man," Muriel said. "By that I mean—"

"Conscientious," Lorca said.

"Definitely," Muriel said.

"We haven't talked finances," Lorca said. "Awkward but necessary, right?"

"My parents left me enough, for the express purpose of buying a house," Muriel said.

"We'd let the bank work out the details, then," Lorca said.

"Well, Zach, we don't want to overstay our welcome," Muriel said. And then, turning to Lorca, "We'll give you our phone number in Brookfield, okay? We'll wait to hear from you."

"No," Lorca said. "I have to go upstairs and lie down now. I'm suddenly quite tired. But, you two, the house is yours if you want it. And why not? My intuition is as good as the next person's."

Muriel and Zachary looked a little stunned. I think they wanted to show more emotion than they allowed themselves. Lorca took the reins in that regard, and embraced them both, and said, "I really must lie down. But please go look at the barn, and maybe take a walk up the road. Whatever you like. I have every confidence that the property and views will help shore up your decision."

Then Lorca went upstairs; I could tell that she didn't want to be seen or to see anyone. Muriel and Zachary did walk up the road, and then they drove off. When, in two hours, Lorca woke, she went downstairs and prepared some tea. Carrying her cup, she began her own private tour, for her own edification, with, "This, of course, is the kitchen. I remember the time Ed sat here and told us about what happened one night when he was captain of the volunteer fire department, and Curtis told about a wild incident she witnessed when she was a journalist in Greece." On and on, in every room, including our bedroom, where she said, "Ahem, well, what went on in here isn't part of the tour."

In the kitchen at about six o'clock, Lorca made a salad. The news was on Vermont Public Radio. She ate the salad standing up, looking out the kitchen window. She then put a bottle of vodka, a bottle of orange juice, and a glass on a tray and carried it up to the master bedroom. But then she decided to lie down in the guest room instead. She mixed a drink and took a few sips, then a more substantial gulp, and set the glass on the bedside table. Rearranging pillows against the headboard, she situated herself comfortably and began to page through a book of Cézanne landscapes. She finished her drink and concocted another, this one heavier on the vodka. "I don't think I've ever felt so tired in my life," she said. It is a mystery why someone would speak out loud to themselves. Lorca was asleep by eight o'clock.

In the morning, she woke at 5:45. Just getting light out. A barred owl called from one of the maples out front. Lorca could hear it all the way around the house — the varied acoustic collaborations of our hill, trees, road, field, barn, wind, and breeze alike. She had slept in her clothes.

She went into the bathroom off our bedroom, peed, washed her hands, splashed water on her face, and patted it dry with a towel. She brushed her teeth, then went downstairs. She ground coffee and sifted it into a #4 paper cone fitted into a glass beaker. She put a kettle of water on the stove. She looked out the window and puttered around, and when the water boiled, she poured it into the cone, waited for it to empty, then filled a mug with coffee, and for the first time I had ever seen, she did not add milk. A small but startling detail to me. She stood looking out the window again.

A moment or two went by. To me, Lorca seemed all alert composure.

"Simon, my darling," she said, still looking out the window. She held her mug in midair. "Whenever you saw that I had something urgent to share, you'd say, 'Just tell me.' So I must tell you, Simon. I've sold our house."

MISSING
ADAMANT
GIRL FOUND

O N THE BULLETIN BOARD in Zachary's office, I read the front-page, March 21, 1995, article in the *Times Argus:*

MISSING ADAMANT GIRL FOUND

Corrine Lily Moore, 11 years old and a resident of Adamant, went missing last year on September 1. This morning, Corrine was found alive at the home of her abductors, in St. Johnsbury.

The Moore family nightmare ended at approximately 6:15 a.m., when officers from the Vermont Bureau of Criminal Investigation, the Vermont State Police and the St. Johnsbury Town Police, warrant in hand, carried out an inspection at the home of Robert Tremain, 39, and his wife Frances, 40. An officer from the VSP found Corrine asleep in an upstairs bedroom. "They had a children's room all set up," said Commander Sidney Benson of the VBCI. "After a brief interrogation, the male suspect admitted he and his wife considered Corrine to be their adopted child." On a preliminary charge of kidnapping, Robert and Frances Tremain are being held in an undisclosed location, pending arraignment. They had been employed by Devon Moore, father of the victim, in his orchid greenhouse in Adamant.

Vermont state law, Statute 13 V.S.A., states: "A person commits the crime of kidnapping if s/he not being a relative of a person under the age of 16 knowingly restrains that person with the intent to keep the person from his or her lawful custodian for a substantial period." The same statute states that kidnapping is punishable by a maximum sentence of life imprisonment.

Corrine's father, Devon, owns Vermont Orchids Co., and her mother, Johanna, is on the faculty at St. Johnsbury Academy. "Within an hour of their reporting their daughter missing, the investigation began," Commander Benson said.

At noon today, in the family kitchen, Devon offered a heartrending chronology. "My wife was teaching at the academy," he said, "and I'd been in the greenhouse. I knew that Corrine was going to walk the short distance to the co-op here in Adamant to buy some apples. She liked to feed apples to our neighbor's horses. After that, she would've had her homeschooling. When her teacher, Karen Zauer, walked into the greenhouse, she said Corrine was nowhere to be found. I ran directly to the co-op — no Corrine. I telephoned all the neighbors. I drove around the roads with Karen for a good hour. Driving back, Karen noticed, to the side of the road, Corrine's field guide to moths, which she never is without. That's when I called the state police. Then I called my wife at the academy. That was no easy call to make."

A focused investigation was handled by Detective Sergeant Owen Corsica, a twenty-eight-year veteran in the VSP. "This was only the fifth missing person case I've been personally involved in," he said, "but my first that involved a missing child. Seeing the look on Mr. and Mrs. Moore's faces when they were reunited with their daughter at Central Vermont Hospital was the reward of a lifetime in law enforcement. All up and down the corridors of CVH, receptionists to nurses, doctors to security, there wasn't a dry eye."

Late this morning, after a mandatory medical examination, Corrine was allowed to return home, where she was met by at least one hundred residents of Adamant and neighboring towns. Speaking to people huddled together in the cold, Johanna Moore said, "Words cannot express the gratitude Devon and I have to everyone who called, visited and offered prayers for our Corrine. Every one of you did all you could to help. We have a truly wonderful community. Our heartfelt thanks to all the intrepid law enforcement personnel. We will thank you individually, believe me. We also wish to thank investigators Zachary Anders and Erica Heilman, of the Green Mountain Agency, who worked night and day to find our daughter."

In addition, the Moores received a telephone call from Senator Patrick Leahy and from Governor Howard Dean.

According to David Vlamick, director of the Green Mountain Agency, the investigation initially had been assigned to Zachary Anders, now a resident of East Calais. Later in the investigation, seasoned investigator Erica Heilman, also of East Calais, was brought in. All in all, they had followed up on over forty leads.

"As it concerns the positive results of the investigation," Mr. Anders said, "two people are most responsible. First, Mrs. De Longhi, of St. Johnsbury. She gave us vital information. Second, freelance investigator Erica Heilman. The best way I can put it is, without their contributions, it might have taken much longer to locate Corrine Moore, which would have continued to cause the Moore family much anguish."

REPORTED BY JACQUELINE WARREN AND

SEABROOK MOODIE

The day of the arrest, Zachary had to stay at his office until 7 p.m. to deal with journalists, follow-up protocol, and paperwork, and for a small celebratory reception in the lobby of the state supreme court. Muriel drove to Montpelier for that, and afterward they had dinner in town. Once back in the farmhouse, Zachary said, "It's finally catching up with me, Murr. I know it's only nine-thirty, but I'm going up to bed."

"You *should* let it catch up with you, Zach. I'll get a bath and be right up." Zachary took two Tylenols and was asleep by ten. Next to him in bed, Muriel read a story by Yasushi Inoue, "Life of a Counterfeiter," until she dozed off with the bedside light on.

Zachary had the next morning off, but had to be in his office by one o'clock. The telephone rang at eight-thirty. Muriel picked it up and drowsily said hello. As she talked on the phone, Zachary went downstairs in pajama bottoms and a T-shirt. He looked into the library and saw Epilogue sitting on the typewriter. He put two logs in the woodstove and, once the fire blazed up, went into the kitchen to prepare coffee. Epilogue was now in the kitchen, moving a plastic bowl an inch or two with his nose and meowing. Zachary fed him and then ground the coffee and got the machine going. He sat in front of the fire, but almost immediately had to get Epilogue off the counter, where he was batting a paw against the glass carafe, maybe attempting to get at the dripping coffee, or maybe jousting with the reflection of the night-light on the glass. Muriel walked into the living room, dressed in sweatpants, sweater, and socks. Epilogue went right up to her, and she said, "Have you been a good boy, Eppy?"

"Muriel, have you ever seen Epilogue drink coffee?"

"Of course not."

"Are you sure? I think he's developed a taste for coffee."

"Come on, really? Can a cat develop a taste for something he hasn't tasted?"

"I think we should test it out."

"Okay, leave a little in a saucer. Let it cool down first, he could burn his tongue."

"It's just a theory about him. He's next to the coffee machine a lot. Hops right up. He did it again just now."

"It's got a lot of moving parts. I think that's what it is."

"I think we should call our vet, ask her about coffee addiction in Maine coon cats."

"You're in a good mood, Zach. I can only imagine how relieved you feel. A huge, huge weight lifted off your shoulders, huh?"

"And yours, really. I'm sorry I zonked out so early."

"I fell asleep with the light on myself."

"Tonight I'm going to read that chapter in the book you brought home. You know the chapter—"

"—how being pregnant can make sex—"

"Yeah."

"Zach, that's sweet, but I think it's referring to a little further along. I'm not going to even show for a while. I think the chapter's more about—"

"Positions."

"Yep."

"Who was on the phone, by the way?"

Zachary brought two cups of coffee into the living room, set them on the table in front of the woodstove, kissed Muriel's forehead, and sat down.

"It was Lorca Pell," Muriel said. "She's coming over this afternoon. I told her you'd be at your office, and she asked that I say congratulations. She said she was in the co-op this morning, and Janet, who makes the papier-mâché animals, had lined up ten papier-mâché woodchucks out front of the store—the woodchucks are on their hind legs—and they're holding a banner, WELCOME HOME, CORRINE, with five exclamation points."

"Lorca must miss the house a lot, is my guess," Zachary said, sipping coffee. "I bet I'll run into her now and then, at the co-op, I mean. Can't wait for it to get warmer. Last September, even early October, I loved sitting at the picnic bench there. The little waterfalls. I guess it's sort of my Zen retreat, as if I really knew what a Zen retreat is."

"Lorca was up at her husband's grave yesterday while everything with Corrine was unfolding. I know she speaks to him. I've heard her because her voice drifts down, if I'm near the stone wall, say."

About two o'clock, Lorca parked her Volvo wagon across the road. Rain was pelting down, the first real deluge announcing the start of mud season. Lorca wore a rain slicker—I was startled to realize it was the one she'd purchased in Point Reyes. The hood was drawn partway over her head. She carried a portfolio carrying case, and on her way to the house, a gust of wind lifted it like a black wing, and she had to secure it with both hands as she walked across the yard to the side porch.

She knocked on the mudroom door, opened it a little, said, "Halloo—hello, it's me, Lorca Pell!" and stepped into the kitchen.

Muriel walked right up and gave Lorca a hug, no matter the wet rain slicker. "So glad you're here," she said. "Unfortunately, Zach's had to go in to work."

"Big, big days for him—for you, too. I can only imagine. Hero husband, huh?"

"Not how he sees himself, believe me. I guess I don't see him that way either. He sees only that it took too long to find Corrine Moore."

"In the co-op, he won't ever have to pay for another scone. Let me put it that way."

This brought on laughter, and then Lorca hung the rain slicker on the coatrack, carried the portfolio into the living room, and said, "Oh, the house looks great, Muriel. There's no such general thing as a woman's touch — there's an individual woman's touch, and what I see is your touch. Really, the house looks wonderful."

"Coffee or tea?"

"I'll have a coffee. I've tried to stop coffee past nine a.m. The exception's maybe an espresso if work's going well. Or badly, for that matter."

Lorca set the portfolio on the dining room table and sat down across from the woodstove. I stood in the front hallway and took in her face, her hands, her whole self, and saw that she had lost weight. I was crazy about her new, shorter haircut, and the fact that her hair was now a slightly darker auburn. But perhaps the hue was informed by dim light, due to the rain and lowered sky through the windows. Epilogue walked over to her for some attention. In a few minutes, Muriel brought in coffee.

They sat at either end of the sofa. "Guess who I saw this morning?" Lorca said. "Corrine Moore. Bright as a bright button, there she was, in a red raincoat and black sou'wester fisherman's hat, that field guide to moths — way too early for moths, of course. It was inside a plastic bag, which she'd fastened to her wrist with a rubber band. Her mother was with her. That's naturally going to take a while, of course."

"You mean for Corrine to walk to the co-op on her own?"

"Yes. But it's great that they got her out into the world first thing, don't you think?"

"I'll tell Zach this evening. That you saw Corrine."

Then Muriel stood up, went into the laundry room, and came back with a folded towel. She unfolded it and said, "Do you mind? I don't want you to catch your death."

"Oh, I can do it, thank you."

"No, allow me, Lorca." And Muriel gently rubbed the towel over Lorca's head, just for a moment.

"Look a little like Rod Stewart, now, do I?" Lorca said.

"I've been thinking of getting mine cut."

They talked for a while, and Muriel asked, "Is your apartment the way you want it now?"

It seemed Lorca recognized this as euphemistic for "How is life?" or wanted to see it that way, and she set her cup down and said, "Well, since Simon died, I can't be totally happy, you know. But I'm reasonably happy, considering. Not sleeping all that well. The BBC is good company. You can find out the day's news six hours ahead of time — okay, now I'm informed — then paint with the classical station on."

"The apartment's comfortable, then."

"Muriel, it was a good thing to sell you the house. You should know, it was a very good decision for me. And, yes, the apartment's next to perfect, and good for the budget. I've got Simon's life insurance tucked away for a rainy day. And I've been working toward a new gallery exhibition."

"Can Zach and I attend?"

"It'll be down in Boston, three months or so."

"Please let us know when and where."

"That's nice. Thank you. In fact, I've brought some drawings to show you. If it's not an imposition. I brought them because they're of the house. Well, mainly of Simon's memorial, which was held right here. A week after he died."

"I'm honored. I'd like very much to see them."

"It's all superficial and it's all clichés when painters talk about what they put into their paintings. I want to scream when I hear such nonsense. I really do. But between you and me and the stars in the sky, I suppose I've put in every possible emotion, crying jags to anger to love, and I continue to love Simon with all my heart. Though we'd drifted apart a little, but that's for another conversation, someday. But no matter, that. He was the love of my life."

"I understand crying jags, Lorca. Though for different reasons, of course."

"Crying jags during Bette Davis movies, and so on. It's like grief — overused word, maybe. It's like grief gives you a kind of arrhythmia. Your heart seems to speed up, then slow down. Completely unrelated to too much coffee. Anyway, I look at these recent drawings and I see the emotions. But nobody in a gallery will see the same ones. In a way, that's good."

"When you're ready, let's look at them," Muriel said.

"Know what I did recently? I paid for a memorial plaque to be put on an armrest of a seat at the Savoy."

"Oh, I've read a lot of those."

"The plaque for Simon's in the back row. If we went to

the movies with other people, he'd sometimes sit back there by himself. If it was just us two, of course he'd sit with me closer up. But if he went by himself, he'd always sit in the back row."

"How is the plaque inscribed?"

"'Simon Inescort—Writer.'"

"Simple is best."

"The plaques started out as a fundraising idea for the theater, and a lot of people got right on board with that. But they must've understood—Rick and Andrea being two of the most perceptive people I know—the plaques would turn out to be a way to memorialize friends and family, or just someone you admired. At first I didn't want to share Simon that way. But then I did."

"I'll look for it next time we're there."

"I've done something else I thought I'd never do. I joined a movie club. We meet at the Savoy, ten a.m. Mondays. The club pays a projectionist. Movies are ordered through a distributor. We pass the hat for all expenses. It feels like an exclusive private screening, as much as it possibly can in Montpelier. After the movie, we all trundle over to a café. That's where the opinions fly, and a lot of good cheer and crankiness. Mostly good cheer, but there's one gal in our group— I don't know what gets into her, but she's like a perpetual Opposites Day."

"Sorry, I'm not getting the reference."

"Oh, sorry, my generation. In elementary school, every Friday was Opposites Day. If somebody stood up and said, 'I'm happy!' another kid was supposed to stand up and cry out, 'Boo-hoo, I'm so sad!' On and on in that fashion. It was all melodrama, and we loved it, and sometimes very surprising things would happen. One time, Everett Sims—I can't believe I still remember his name—Everett stood up and said, 'My mother and dad live in separate houses now.' But nobody could come up with an opposite for that. Another time, Susan Wherity said, 'I'm afraid of the drawer with the manila paper in it!' and Gary Van Eerden ran over to the manila paper drawer, took out a piece, and started eating it! I kid you not, and he was making lion growls and tearing it apart with his teeth. I think this was meant to be courtship on Gary's part. The teacher, Mrs. Botton, started to shout, 'Verbal! Verbal! Verbal!' since you were only supposed to *say* opposite things, not *do* them. But too late, Gary Van Eerden was throwing up on Mrs. Botton's desk. He had to go to the nurse's room."

"So you've got an oppositional person in your movie club, I take it."

"Yes, sorry for the tangent there. Yes, her name's Alice Comb. Comb spelled as in comb your hair. She does watercolors and cloying poems for Hallmark cards, down in Thetford, and drives up for the movies, undeterred by weather, which is admirable. So for instance, we watched a real tearjerker last time. All the hardest hearts went to mush, including Alice's, by the way. I sat next to her, and let me tell you, *Dark Victory* did us all in. You know it? With Bette Davis?"

"I've noticed it was playing on TV, but I haven't seen it."

"Bette's a savvy, impetuous young socialite with an inoperable brain tumor. Talk about pushing all your buttons! Both George Brent and Humphrey Bogart are in love with her, different styles of going about it, but still. At one point Bette says, 'Moving to Vermont are you? What do you do there in between yawns?' Plus, *Dark Victory* was made in 1939. Just think what was going on in the world then. The movie has big operatic feelings, and like I said, even Alice fell apart. But at brunch, Alice was suddenly all snickers. What I felt was, Alice hasn't had any romance in her life for thirty years, so no wonder that Bette Davis flick sets her off."

Muriel set down her cup. "I'd love to join. It's probably a pretty exclusive group. I mean, old, dear friends. But if there's an opening, would you recommend me?"

"Muriel, a professor like you? Writing books. All sorts of things going on. I'm surprised you'd have the time, no matter the inclination."

"I love movies. And we could drive in together, maybe. Anyway, it'd be nice for me. I'm no film scholar, I just like the movies. I'm not oppositional, either."

"Alice already fills that personality slot, right? Yes, of course, I'll mention you next time we meet, which is . . . I forgot when. I'd be happy to. Oh, good."

"Which movie is next?"

"That I do know. It's *The Letter.* I suggested it, my turn. And I confess it's kind of an obsession with me, *The Letter.*"

"What's it about, generally?"

"It's another Bette Davis. To my mind, it's got the scariest ending of all time, in the atmosphere sense and, well, no details, but Bette gets done in. It's a Somerset Maugham story. Somerset Maugham adored Bette Davis, I once read."

Muriel placed her hand over Lorca's hand and said, "Lorca,

I'm pregnant—oh, my Lord. I promised not to say anything for the requisite three months. I haven't told anyone else. Except Zach, of course."

"Neither will I. It's wonderful news. Maybe it's this farmhouse."

"How do you mean?"

"Oh, anyone can see you and Zachary are like two peas in a pod. I know I already told you some of this, but the Peck family built this house. And the maple trees out front, each one was named after a Peck daughter—Charlotte, Irene, and Helen. And the library was the birthing room."

"The Pecks provided good karma, then," Muriel said.

"I'm certain that's true for you and Zachary. You know, Muriel, every little thing Simon and I did, fixed this and that, the screened porch added, the new roof, it just felt right. We wanted to be thoughtful about it, as if Will Peck and his family were watching. Maybe 'respectful' is the word. We felt it kept a connection between centuries, is how Simon put it. I know that's got a certain sentimentality to it, but it's how we felt."

"Me and Zach have read everything you left us to read about the house. It really means a lot."

"You'll live how you want to live here. You'll construct memories completely your own. I do miss the house every day, but I would've been miserable here alone. What I'm trying to say is, it just feels right to speak personally about things with you. I don't expect a deep friendship, Muriel, but if that's to happen, we have the house to thank for it. That's how I look at it. Not to worry, though. I'm not the sort to be a burden. I'll continue to visit Simon, naturally. But that ghost clause I told you about, in the original deed? I'm not going to haunt the house so you have to activate the ghost clause and I'll have to buy back the house, according to the law!"

They both laughed. Lorca took a sip of coffee and said, "My grandmother, who lived by the ocean, used to say, when plovers would return every year. She used to say, 'Home-sickness guides them back.' She meant homesickness was a natural and very powerful thing."

"I like that a lot."

"Well, I suppose widowhood—and I'm a fairly young widow, aren't I? I suppose it's no stranger than any situation in life. It's certainly different. It's staggeringly difficult, nights especially. The other day, a friend of mine said you can be excruciatingly lonely even living with someone. Well, platitude or not, that sort of relativism can help a little. Not a lot, but a little. Oh, I've said too much."

"Everything said here is *entre nous*."

"I'm most fortunate, all the dear, good friends I have. I've got money to live on. Still, there's been tests of will, I guess you might call them. For example, I've got this . . . what to call him? An acquaintance. Dear and intelligent man. Name is Charles. I never much gave him the time of day when Simon was alive. There weren't many opportunities, really. But I've since met with him twice for coffee in town. Both times I wasn't my most composed. The conversations weren't without interest, even tenderness, but then my temper would flare. I'd bring personal feelings to rather neutral subjects. He kept saying, well, we really don't know each other. My pissy aggressiveness owning to sorrow, I suppose."

"Of course it's owning to sorrow," Muriel said.

"Shrinks call it transference."

"It's a familiar term to me. I read some in psychology."

"I'm *transferring*—I get some of this lingo from a therapist in Williston I've been seeing. Apparently, I'm transferring a lot of unresolved things that me and Simon never quite settled. The word 'grief' is just so fucking inadequate. I mean, try as you might not to cause a near stranger pain, you cause them pain. Which in turn causes you yourself pain."

"All you've been through. Besides, you can't be a good person every minute. You have to forgive yourself. Does that sound, I don't know, too much like inane self-help spiritual bullshit?"

"A little, but still nice to hear. It's all been kind of schizoid. Just last week, I found myself being kind to Vanessa at the co-op. Who could be a real shrew to Simon. And while I might otherwise, when Simon first died, have said to her, 'What a goddamn shrew you were to my husband,' a couple of days ago I ended up saying, 'Thanks for bringing scones to Simon's memorial.' You may not know how horrible her scones taste."

"How horrible are they?"

"Put cardboard and flour the cat peed in, toss in the blender, add lemon or cranberries to taste."

"I'll remember to ask Zach not to bring home scones."

"May I show you the drawings?"

"Please. Let's set them out on the dining room table. I'll take the tablecloth off."

There were twenty drawings in all, each the same size. From experience looking at Lorca's work, I knew their dimensions were nine by twelve inches. They were done in pencil and charcoal. "All of them are of Simon's memorial —you'll recognize the downstairs rooms here."

"When was the memorial, if I may ask?"

"One week after Simon died. You knew he had a heart attack on the ferry to Nova Scotia. He fell over the rail, my poor husband did, and they had to lower a lifeboat— improperly named in this case. Three crew members retrieved him and got him back on the ferry, and they turned around and returned to Bar Harbor. I accompanied Simon from Bar Harbor to the funeral home in Montpelier. In a week, our neighbor David, up the road, built the stone wall —in a week, it was really something. The haiku was chiseled later on the gravestone."

"I love that haiku."

"Anyway, these are all drawings of the memorial potluck."

Muriel and Lorca looked at the drawings, and so did I. As Lorca took each one out, placed it on the table, described the scene depicted, then returned the drawing to the portfolio case, the memorial came back to me with pure vividness.

The first drawing was quite unusual, in the sense that it was the only self-portrait I'd ever seen Lorca do. Self-portrait only in that it included Lorca sitting on the living room sofa, listening to our friend Bill talk about how I'd hang out for hours in his bakery, talking about Eastern European literary history and music. Lorca had given herself a pensive expression. She's dressed in black—the charcoal especially nuanced on her mourning dress, which, in fact, was a dress she wore to a funeral three years earlier—that of the cellist Mario Civitello, who'd also had a heart attack and drowned while swimming in the small pond across from the Adamant Music School, the day after he played Bach's unaccompanied cello suites in the small performance hall. A drawing of Rick sitting in one of the rocking chairs; I remember he played a Cape Breton dirge of some vintage on his fiddle, and Franklin joined in on the pennywhistle for some following improvisation. A drawing of Alexandra and Erica in conversation by the front hallway.

There was a drawing of my oldest, dearest friend, another David, reading my favorite poem of his, "Wavelength." I recall standing in the corner by the front window, feeling overwhelmed by that. A drawing of Rhea holding a plate of food and listening intently—maybe to the poem, or the music, it couldn't be known. A drawing of Steve, a master chef of Chinese cuisine, carrying in a tray of food; Lorca made sure to draw in detail the food Steve had cooked that Sunday afternoon in our kitchen. A drawing of Julie laughing with Jody, Roy and Gabrielle behind them. A drawing of a drawing Ed did, of the two of us sitting together at the table of our favorite café in town; my bowl is filled to the brim with Ed's signature scruffy people in miniature, with outsized proboscises, untamable hair, and bemused expressions, and the caption reads, "I see you ordered today's special." In the drawing, as it was during the memorial, the cartoon is propped up on one of Lorca's wooden easels.

One drawing depicted my Virginia friend, Wyatt, reading a Robert Frost poem, I can't recall which, but a good choice.

The last drawing, titled at the bottom *Visitation,* was a view through the front window. Two of the maples could be seen. There is an enigmatic figure standing next to one of the trees. Muriel bent close to study it. She ran a light finger under the printed title. "This one's all wishful thinking, of course," Lorca said. "That somehow Simon's still close by. Wishful thinking, huh?"

Later, after Lorca had left, I recalled that during the five or so hours of the memorial, with all those friends at the farmhouse, I hadn't wished to eavesdrop. For the most part, I'd always taken at face value what people said to me when I was alive. At the farmhouse that afternoon and evening I didn't care to experience praise, betrayal (doubtful), or anything else. That all those busy lives were devoted to this part of village life seemed generous enough. Some people liked me, and I knew some maybe not so much; some enjoyed my books; some proved inventively cordial toward them. It yet again occurred to me that everything I loved most happened almost every day in Vermont, and now I added my own memorial. Curmudgeon and self-appointed doyenne of the co-op, Vanessa Sprague, had brought a tray of her scones, so I guess I was, in her own way, forgiven; though I took note that my favorite flavor, cranberry, was absent, so maybe I wasn't completely forgiven. Lorca, rising above all past slights and grievances, tapped her glass with a spoon and offered a toast: "To Vanessa, who first told Simon and me about this house, where we had such a full life." There were many other toasts and anecdotes to follow.

Around dusk—I remember the crepuscular light—close-by neighbors drifted up the road. A few walked along the mown path to the grave, where they lingered a moment or two. Small enclaves of conversation formed in the library, living room, dining room, kitchen. Even upstairs in one of the guest rooms, people sat and talked. Rick and Franklin took up their instruments again. By eight o'clock, Alexandra, Deb, Rhea, and Sandra had cleared the dishes and were having coffee in the kitchen. I could see that Lorca was exhausted, and all sorts of other things, too, unnamable, at least by me. She sat at the kitchen table with the others. By ten o'clock, Lorca was alone in the house, except for Alexandra, who thought it best she stay over. They talked until just after midnight.

About seven the next morning, I was sitting in my cabin. I don't think I was thinking; I was staring at the crabapple trees receiving the first light of day, and soon they seemed ignited by the sun. Lorca appeared, wearing pajamas under her jeans, a sweater, and her favorite, if threadbare, sherpa-lined vest. She was holding a cup of coffee, which steamed out into the chill air. As she spoke, I could see her breath. She stood in front of the gravestone and said:

"Well, my dearest, things yesterday went pretty well, I thought. Alexandra spent the night and is going to tonight, too. I don't quite know in which order to tell you things. So I'll just start.

"First, I got the official report—I've tucked it away in a

drawer. But do you know what? Included in the report is a sort of eyewitness account, which surprised me. Just a couple of sentences, but it meant the world to me. It turns out that one of the deckhands on the ferry had been on the deck above you, and said you were both looking at dolphins. This was such precious information to me. And I'm thinking that whoever wrote up this report, with its official language, its facts, whoever wrote this must've known it'd be precious information to me. This is a guess, but I think it's true. The same deckhand reported that you climbed, or seemed to, right up over the rail. Considering the medical report, darling, I can only assume you were somehow climbing to get away from the pain. Or something like that. But you know what really made me laugh? Yes, even though it was about you dying, what made me laugh was the deckhand noting that you wore a life vest. My husband, great reader of Joseph Conrad, worried a sudden gust would fling him overboard. But that vest must have kept you afloat till the lifeboat arrived, right?

"As for yesterday's gathering. Oh my, what to tell you? Well, Vanessa said she never understood a word you wrote. I don't think this necessarily meant she'd ever read any word you ever wrote. Alice said, 'That first novel of Simon's is the one I liked.' These things would've cracked you up. You would've said, 'Village life!' I can just hear you saying it. The way I looked at it, all obtuseness was loving. All I know, Simon, is that a lot of people who attended didn't really want to leave. Deb and Steve, they drove off early, but guess what? They came back and stayed for a couple more hours."

Lorca stepped into my cabin, emerged holding a blanket

that was on the sofa in there, set it on the ground, and sat down. She tossed the remainder of her coffee out onto the grass. She sat there for a good half hour, eyes closed, as if taking a nap, and indeed, maybe she did sleep a little.

"Oh, Simon," she finally said, "we had a good marriage with some difficult things in it. We began two or three marriages within the one we had, is a way to think about it. We stayed in it. How could we know how many hours were left to us? Would we, anyway, have done anything different? Last night, you came to me, but your voice was all radio static — maybe that transistor radio from Point Reyes, do you think? I'm so terrible at analyzing dreams. But you brought me coffee, like every normal morning."

She sat a while longer. Now there was a lot of birdsong. Looking down at the farmhouse, I could see Alexandra standing next to the hummingbird feeder, looking up toward the cabin, then going back inside the house. At my graveside, Lorca said, "Oh, almost forgot, the *Times Argus* printed your obit. Rhea helped me write it." She reached into her vest pocket and took out the clipping, straightened it against her knee, and read.

> The novelist Simon Inescort, age 48, a resident of East Calais, died on May 23. According to his wife, Lorca Pell Inescort, the cause of death was heart failure. En route to Halifax, Nova Scotia, for literary employment, Mr. Inescort fell from the rail of the ferry, out in the Atlantic Ocean, where his body was retrieved by crew members using a lifeboat.
>
> Introducing him several years ago at the Boston Public Library, novelist Jessmyn Chine remarked that Mr. Inescort was a "writer's writer." Mr. Inescort's wife said, "Si-

mon thought this was damning with faint praise, but that any praise is rare enough, and much appreciated. That was my husband's humor."

Sales fluctuated radically from book to book, yet during his career he was once nominated for a National Book Award. *The Plovers* was translated into six languages. Critic Andrew Howorth, in the *Los Angeles Times,* wrote, "*The Plovers* is an only slightly flawed gem of a novel." Mr. Inescort's novella, *I Was Devoted,* was made into an independent film, starring the Canadian actress Megan Follows. It was screened at the Toronto Film Festival.

Mr. Inescort's novels garnered generally positive reviews. He served as writer-in-residence at the University of California, Santa Cruz, and gave a number of public readings. Yet he never attained the heights of popularity that marked the careers of other writers of his generation. Lorca Pell Inescort said, "Simon was pleased to have the readership he had, and his perspective was, writing is a great life and a tough business."

Mr. Inescort was born in Toledo, Ohio, and raised in Michigan and near Toronto, Ontario. He had lived with his wife in Vermont since 1979. In an essay for the *New York Review of Books,* Martha Weiss wrote, "Considering that in the main his novels are set in Canada's easternmost provinces, Inescort, ironically, might be considered a regionalist, but one who does not live in the region he writes about. This is perhaps the consummate example of geographical displacement of the narrative imagination."

Mr. Inescort is survived by his wife, the painter Lorca Pell Inescort. He was known as a devoted husband and devoted friend. He served on the Kellogg-Hubbard Library's board of directors from 1987 to 1989.

Donations may be made to the Simon Inescort Memorial Fund at the Kellogg-Hubbard Library.

"All right, my darling, I'm going back to the house now," Lorca said. "I'll come up again this afternoon. And who knows, maybe once in between, too."

As for the obituary, I thought, Lorca is nothing if not honest, and of the necessarily reductive summary of a life, I thought, fair enough.

MOTHS
COME OUT
OF THE TREES

APRIL 7, 1996 — today sunrise was at 6:31 a.m. There is still need of the woodstoves. From the kitchen, I can see various configurations of spruce and pines along Max Grey Road across the valley, and in the valley, plumes of mist. To the north, a zeppelin-shaped cloud has a swirl of mixed pastel light inside. To the south, out over the general store, the church, the scatter of houses, and the post office, the air is clear as if we should live forever — that is from a poem of W. S. Merwin's. Of course, when the time comes, I will miss Lorca most, but I will also miss the pale light, which some mornings seems to emanate from the beech and birch trees. Epilogue has become oddly more attentive to the space I inhabit.

"Eppy's been pawing in the air when he sits on the rocking chair in the library," Muriel said one morning. "And he's got a new voice — that *aaack-aaack* thing he does, that has the Morse code cadence to it."

"Yeah, I've heard that for a few weeks now," Zachary said. "Maybe he swallowed the sensor under the rug."

"The vet says cats never stop developing vocally."

I feel I am still married to Lorca, very much married to her. Most hours have familiar emotional textures. But I can't touch and feel my corporeal life to the extent I did a year ago. There's been a definite existential shift: the phrase "in the hours still left" never leaves me now.

When I begin to fade, as surely I will — for some reason, I picture a white long-sleeve shirt carried off by the wind over a slow-moving river, merely the latest image I have had, as if auditioning for my next incarnation — besides missing Lorca, I will also miss seeing a fox loping boldly down the snowy dirt road, or the way a crow, as it crosses the wide field behind the farmhouse, hardly flapping a wing, indicates the updrafts. My beloved diarist Edward Lear wrote, "In the morning, look out and let the landscape take up full residence in your heart before all is intervened by the sound of human voices." I will miss experiencing that very thing.

Just now, I've heard Muriel and Zachary's daughter, Elizabeth Rose Streuth Anders, crying softly in her room, Muriel's footsteps from the bedroom, Zachary's from his office, where he was up early working on a new case. Both of them speaking just above a whisper.

My thinking has become not exactly epigrammatic, but more associational. Maybe I am becoming a charcoal drawing. In the hours still left to me, how to explain this? For some reason, starting at around one o'clock this morning, sitting in the library, I felt that each passing moment contained a powerful sense of elegiac anticipation. "Oh exhausting, interminable composition of this life" — that is Lear again. I never thought I, even writing in ghost first person, would register those words on paper, but there you go, the exhausting, interminable composition of this life.

That time I half joked at dinner with friends that I was envious of people who have repressed memories. Well, now, as memories arrive one after the next, I feel I am becoming almost entirely composed of them. It's as if I'm standing in the field out back and my own private drive-in movie screen is there and I have no choice as to which moments in the past are projected onto it.

Take, for instance, something that happened one day last summer. On August 15, Zachary had come home late in the afternoon from working a case that involved the theft of a truckload of encyclopedias, dictionaries, and other reference books intended for schools; the truck was believed to have crossed state lines. Muriel, five months pregnant, poured him a glass of lemonade and said, "I dropped by the co-op to pick up lemonade, some lemons, and a couple of frozen flatbreads. Guess who I ran into? Corrine Moore, Devon, Johanna, and Johanna's sister, Birdy."

"I wonder what 'Birdy' is short for?" Zachary asked.

"Ruby-throated hummingbird, maybe? Or chipping sparrow?"

"Ha ha ha."

"At the co-op, while Vanessa was ringing me up, Johanna said, 'Muriel, so glad we ran into you. I was going to telephone. Corrine has a favor to ask, don't you, honey?' But Corrine was up on a stepladder, plucking a moth from the top shelf of cereals. She got one off a box of shredded wheat, I noticed. She studied it a moment and then let it go free outside. You know how she does."

"I've never seen it myself, but yes."

"Johanna tells me it's Corrine's birthday today, and since we have such a big field out back, would we mind if her family has a get-together near the woods. Just for an hour or two, she said. I asked what she had in mind — just out of curiosity. 'Well, let me show you,' she said. She picks up Corrine's trusty field guide to moths, opens it up, and in the first few pages, she shows me a section called 'How to See Moths.' The long and the short of her request is that one of Corrine's birthday presents would be to come over this evening and set up a white sheet and a special light. It's supposed to attract all sorts of moths right out of the woods. They did this a few times before and it worked like magic, Johanna said."

"Of course you said yes."

"Yes, I said yes. They'll be here, including Aunt Birdy, by seven-fifteen."

"I think we should roast marshmallows," Zachary said.

"Great idea."

"I'm driving right now to the general store for marshmallows. Then I'll whittle some sticks. Mr. Outdoors, huh?"

Zachary returned with two packages of marshmallows, which he set on the kitchen table. He went outside, and I watched him gather some thin branches from the pear tree that a recent storm had knocked to the ground. He carried the branches to the house, and with a jackknife whittled them into sticks, the ends blunted. Corrine, Devon, Johanna, and Birdy arrived a little late, around 7:30. On the road out front of the farmhouse, first thing, before introductions were made, Birdy said, "A lot of people ask, but 'Birdy' isn't short for anything. That's my whole original first name, Birdy."

"Nice to meet you, Birdy," Muriel said, smiling over at Zachary.

Corrine was dressed in shorts and ankle-high red tennis shoes and held her field guide. I noticed Zachary staring at her, and it occurred to me it was the first time he'd actually laid eyes on Corrine since the morning she was rescued in St. Johnsbury. He walked up, held out his hand, and Corrine shook hands with him as he said, "Hi. I'm Zach."

Corrine walked over to the house and looked in through a library window for a few minutes. Then she took a few steps to her right and looked in through another library window.

"Is Karen Zauer homeschooling again this fall?" Muriel asked Johanna.

"We're lucky to have her," Johanna said. "We've got a special curriculum worked out. We try to arrange a lot of play-dates, too. Some of those work better than others. Other children, bless their hearts, don't quite know how to interact with Corrine, and vice versa. All this is some unusual education, I can tell you that. Devon and I have come a long ways, except the road's endless. Yesterday Corrine went on her own to the co-op, and to feed apples to the neighbor's horses. It's been a good active summer. Oh well, now's not the time for my chatter, is it? It's Corrine's birthday."

Muriel walked over to Corrine and said, "We've got a birthday present for you."

Muriel went into the farmhouse and brought out a gift-wrapped box. She looked at Zachary, whose expression suggested, *Whatever you came up with, it's fine by me.* Muriel held out the box for Corrine. Corrine handed her mother the field guide, took the box, and walked to the nearby picnic bench to open it. Muriel had given Corrine a luna moth mounted inside a black-framed glass display case. Zachary almost certainly would've recalled that it was an heirloom from Muriel's grandmother. For a moment, it felt as if a current of tense anticipation ran through everyone, worry about how Corrine might respond to a moth she couldn't set free. That was, I admit, my own concern. But Corrine said, *"Actias luna."* Hearing this, Devon and Johanna didn't blink an eye, whereas Zachary and Muriel looked at each other with incredulousness.

Johanna then read from the field guide: "Apple green wings are marked with sleepy-looking elliptical eyespots outlined yellow, white, and black . . . Has dramatically long, slightly twisted tails. Hosts: deciduous trees, including alder, beech, cherry, hazelnut, hickory, and willow."

It was getting very near dusk. Everyone walked up past the cabin except for Devon, who'd returned to his car, taken out the equipment he needed, then caught up with the rest in the high field, about thirty or so yards from the woods. Zachary carried a small satchel full of kindling, matches, the whittled sticks, the marshmallows, a flashlight, and a plastic bottle of water, clearly just to be safe, even with a small campfire. Inside the stone wall, Corrine lifted a moth from my gravestone and let it go, and it flitted directly back to the gravestone, where she let it be. She didn't recite its Latin name, and I thought, Come on, she can't possibly know them all. But I may have been very wrong about that. What did I know, anyway, about how Corrine's mind worked?

Everyone had climbed up the slope of the field, through tall, bristly weeds and grass, until Devon called out, "This is close enough, I think!" The birches were closest, just on the other side of a stone wall, with what looked like mortar of moss and lichen between the stones. A kestrel swooped downslope, chased by crows, but I couldn't tell if anyone else noticed. Nature always seemed somehow intensified at dusk, or that was my experience at least. Crepuscular light could bring on this sensation. So, there everyone was, and Zachary scuffed a bare spot out with the heel of his shoe, yanked up grass in handfuls until there was a clear site for a fire. He set out a little kindling, ignited it with a match, then added some larger sticks. It all flared nicely, and Zachary then added a small log from the stack inside the house. Now things were all set for roasting marshmallows.

Devon had rigged a basic scaffolding and draped a bed-sheet over it. Behind the sheet, he set up a black-light CFL bulb, which was clamped to a tripod. "That about does it," he said. "The whole rigmarole came to just thirty-six dollars plus change. I already had the tripod. The sheet's from our linen closet."

Zachary handed out the whittled sticks, each with a marshmallow stuck to the end. He fixed one for himself, too. Everyone sat in a circle around the fire, Corrine between Johanna and Devon. She hadn't uttered a word since she'd given the Latin name of the luna moth. But now she said, "When are they coming?"

"It's not quite dark yet, sweetie pie," Devon said. "Just wait."

Corrine said, "Wait wait wait wait wait."

The marshmallows were completely gone in less than half an hour. The oaks and pines that stretched for a good quarter mile along the stone wall were hidden by the dark now, in a way the white birches would never be. "I think it's time," Devon said. "What with only a small stand of evergreens last time we did this, we had a lot of luck. So with this big field and woods, I have high hopes." He stood up, walked behind the sheet, and switched on the black light. With that, the sheet held a penumbra, blue on the inside, its outer circle white.

"Through that sheet," Birdy said, "that tripod looks like an alien."

"Birdy!" Johanna said. "We're here for birthday moths, remember? Not aliens."

"I stand corrected," Birdy said.

Corrine, Johanna, Muriel, and Birdy stood on one side of the sheet, while on the other side stood Zachary holding the flashlight, Devon, and myself. Suddenly, from about twenty yards back in the direction of the cabin, Lorca called out, "Sorry I'm late — it's me, Lorca." When she reached the others, she said, "Thanks for inviting me. This is special." She smoothed some insect repellent along her arms, patted some on her forehead and behind her neck, even dabbed some on her wrists, like perfume. I'd say it was another twenty minutes before the first moths appeared on the sheet. And in fact, they seemed to have arrived out of nowhere, so either no one had noticed or no one had called out their approach. Corrine walked up to Zachary, took the flashlight, and shined the light at the sheet, illuminating one individual moth after the next. Soon there were several groups of three or four clustered together, perhaps twenty in all, distributed mainly within the penumbra, though a few were outliers. A number of moths flitted about the tripod behind the sheet, too, and their dancing silhouettes could be seen through it. Corrine switched off the flashlight and faced the trees.

"Our daughter will now greet the *arrivants* and *arrivantes,*" Johanna said.

"My wife's got two years of high school French," Devon said.

"Look, there!" Muriel called out, pointing to her left. "There, there, there!" It was possible to track a large dark moth as it fluttered past Corrine and fastened itself to the sheet. Corrine again clicked on the flashlight and pointed its shaft of light toward the woods. It was as though the spectral world was sending its myriad emissaries. Moth after moth after moth. Within an hour and a half, the light and sheet had drawn at least two hundred. "This is working just like the book said it should work," Devon said. I could tell there were dozens of different species.

"Isn't this the best birthday?" Johanna said.

Corrine stood to one side, reeling off, nearly sotto voce, Latin names right and left, gleefully, but not lifting a single moth from the sheet. She then took ten or twelve steps toward the trees and shone the flashlight ahead. "Stay home, stay home!" she said, crying a little. There was a definite sense of alarm in her voice.

Lorca had stood a little apart, but now was beside Corrine, who handed her the flashlight.

Corrine was becoming agitated. She took Lorca's hand and they walked back to the sheet. There, Corrine said, "Mom, they're all feeling lost."

"You're absolutely right," Johanna said. "That's very nice of you, sweet girl." Johanna looked at Devon, and he immediately began to dismantle everything, first shaking the moths out into the night.

"That all was better than fireworks!" Birdy said.

After the Moore family drove off in their car, Lorca stayed for a late dinner. "How about frittatas and a beer, Lorca?" Muriel said. "Frittatas are one of Zach's favorites."

"Sounds delicious," Lorca said.

THAT IS THE MEMORY of Corrine's birthday and of those moths having appeared as if from the spectral world, which I'm presently a citizen of.

What I have, really, is the ongoingness of things observed in the house. Now Elizabeth is a lively, so far even-tempered two-year-old who loves to watch classic Buster Keaton skits and who cannot tolerate Dr. Seuss books, which she pushes away. Finally, Zachary gave all their Dr. Seuss to the Kellogg-Hubbard children's room. But otherwise, Lizzy demands a minimum of three books at bedtime. If offered just two picture books, she's capable of throwing her indestructible plastic owl-face clock across the room, and laughing.

Zachary has had a stretch of what he calls run-of-the-mill cases. Yet that has to be a relative statement, considering the search for Corrine Moore was his first assignment at the Green Mountain Agency. On the other hand, "an alcoholic lowlife waved a gun in the window when I held up a warrant for overdue alimony," he'd told Muriel, who said, "Did I need to know that?"

This exchange upset her, and it upset him to see her upset, and the incident itself, he later admitted, had felt harrowing as it unfolded: the guy actually shot a window out.

One night, when they were discussing Zachary's work, Muriel said, "This is something I could only share with you, darling. But the other night—and I don't know why that night—I started to say prayers again. Not the Lord's Prayer. No, apparently I've come up with my own style. It's all having to do with Lizzy. I just ask, outright, that she keep her good health. Nothing more, nothing less. Minimalist prayers. I include you and me sometimes, too."

"Do you include our marriage?"

"All one and the same. You, me, Elizabeth—that's our marriage. But I don't want you to think, because of what happened with that alimony guy, I'm all of a sudden obsessed by mortality or anything like that. I'm not. I do now and then take a deep breath. Like you say, 'I'm a professional.' Okay, I'm getting all Eeyore here, aren't I? Did I tell you about Kazumi and Ardith? To change the subject."

"How are they? I haven't seen them in ages."

"They're wanting to get married."

"Tell me."

"The legal getting married part?"

"No, first the relationship part."

"Ardith proposed and Kazumi said yes. To some, it

might've happened fast. But both had wanted to fall in love for so long, Zach."

"They're extremely good friends to you, Murr. I'm liking them each and together a lot. Not that I feel I really know them yet. But as you know, I'm slow to declare friendships. That's just me. Is Ardith having luck finding a teaching position?"

"She's got interviews. One in Boston, I think. Which would mean a commute, but not a terrible one."

"I wouldn't like it."

"I have a commute, don't forget. To teaching and back. But as for the marriage part, they're researching if there's any countries that allow same-gender marriages. Can they get married in Hungary, say, if they're US citizens? Plus, they have to find out which states acknowledge foreign same-gender marriages. All like that. They've got a difficult road. They're intrepid and want this and belong together, and that's that. From what I can tell, they are combining all their fortitudes."

"Add them to your prayers. I don't mean that facetiously, either."

"Kazumi's going to chair her department next year. If they stay in Portsmouth."

"Big raise in pay, department chair, right?"

"I didn't ask, but I assume so."

"Forgot to mention, I ran into Lorca at the co-op. I was picking up bread. She said she's available to babysit Friday. There's that movie at the Savoy, right?"

"Czech bohemian artists love story, is how it's being touted."

"Remember, I don't like movies that too much resemble my own life."

"Ha ha, very funny. Can we go to Langdon Street Tavern after? Celebrate my teaching award, remember?"

"Talk about a raise."

"Fifteen hundred a year. Enough to keep us in onions."

"And you're liking your present students so much. That's nice, isn't it?"

"None of them as interesting as Ardith Paleo. But that bar is high in terms of interestingness. Is that even a word?"

WHAT ELSE?

In death I shall continue to have literary affections, which is from Maupassant, *and in the meantime, I shall not let a single hour be given to dispassion.* That is my new mantra. If these are the final hours given to me, I won't let one be given to dispassion.

The catalog of Lorca's recent exhibition is on Muriel's desk. Four framed photographs of Elizabeth are on the piano.

On the days I spend time in my cabin, I often wonder why neither Lorca, earlier, nor Muriel and Zachary, once they owned the house, haven't cleared it out. Probably it just hasn't been a priority. Besides, there's nothing notable in the cabin except some books, a poster of Isabelle Huppert in *The Lacemaker,* an old sagging sofa, a Canadian school desk and chair, a manual typewriter. And a radio.

Then, one evening, when Muriel and Zachary held bowls of lamb stew, and Lizzie was eating Jell-O, and they were watching Buster Keaton shorts, I heard Muriel say, "Do you think we should turn the cabin into a guest cottage? I asked Chet, who's a jack-of-all-trades, and he said putting a small bathroom up there wouldn't be too big a deal. The propane stove keeps it nice and cozy in the winter, right? We could put in a big bed. The view's amazing. Trees and stone walls wherever you look."

"Kazumi and Ardith could use it weekends."

"I know you feel the house is a little crowded when they're here."

"A little."

"God knows, they prefer Vermont to New Hampshire."

"Would they mind sleeping so close to Simon Inescort, do you think?"

"Kazumi's started a new book about Osamu Dazai, a famous suicide. Great moody writer. So I think the single-occupant cemetery might even be an inspiration."

"Weird, but sounds right. So does a guest cottage. I think we should run the idea by Lorca. It just seems proper etiquette."

"She'll say the house is ours, do what we wish."

"Still, it's only right."

Lorca arrived to babysit at 5:30, because Muriel and Zachary wanted to provide her an early dinner and chat awhile. The movie was at 7:00. Zachary served her up some of the lamb stew from the Dutch oven. When Lorca finished eating, she opened a portfolio of drawings to show. Holding Lizzy, who was dressed in pajamas with feet, her curly red hair frizzed up from a bath, Muriel looked at the drawings while Zachary went upstairs to make a phone call before they left. The drawings were again charcoal and pencil. There were six in all. Each showed a couple sitting at a kitchen table. The lines were elegant; the faces had succinct expressions. On the shelf behind them, a Morandi-like tableau of vases. "These are from a new series," Lorca said.

I stood at the kitchen window. A few starlings and one goldfinch were at the feeder; westerly out toward the Green Mountains, three enormous clouds displayed dark updrafts; a caravan of wild turkeys was moving across the back field, between the apple trees and the opposite stone wall; though not yet visible, the moon somehow felt near; the air was clear as if we should live forever. I suddenly recalled being at the rail of the ferry. I wore that life vest. I tasted the salt in the wind. There were a dozen or so dolphins racing alongside. It was a thrilling sight. I do recall thinking, Lorca would love seeing these dolphins. For some reason, I turned and looked up and saw a deckhand, who appeared to be looking at the dolphins, too. I waved and he waved back. I turned back to the rail. The dolphins were quite close to the ferry now; I had to lift myself up and lean a little over the rail to see them. I heard myself say, "Oh." A knifing pain rolled from my heart to my shoulder. I remember falling. I remember seeing dolphins as I fell. I remember the shocking coldness of the sea.

"What's this series called?" Muriel asked.

"*Dialogues on the Greater Harmonies,*" Lorca said.

"May I ask why?"

"Oh, it's how Simon referred to our breakfast conversations. Of course, they weren't any such lofty thing at all. No, we talked to each other just like any other couple having difficulties, but keeping those apart from a lovely breakfast as best we could."

Lorca took Lizzie in her arms, and Lizzie seemed quite comfortable with this.

"I'll go up and get ready, then," Muriel said.

"You have a good time in town. I'll be interested in your opinion of the movie. I was thinking of seeing it myself."

THE
FARMHOUSE

Today I was considering how, within the ongoingness of an old farmhouse, getting used to things doesn't mean a lack of constant adjustments. For instance, of late, Zachary has been obsessing—yet again—about the MOTION IN LIBRARY situation, whereas for the last few months Muriel has said things like, "I don't care how, really, but I just want to be shut of it." The sensor under the Turkish rug is connected again these days. Yet during much of February and March of Elizabeth's third year it had been disconnected. Connected or disconnected, the MOTION IN LIBRARY signal kept getting sent at unpredictable moments to Onion River Security. Of the occasional discussions I've heard Muriel and Zachary have about this subject, none appeared to come to a painful point, though a few definitely underscored contrasts in their basic natures.

"Okay, well, obviously I'm an investigator," Zachary said one night when they were having an early dinner. Elizabeth was next door playing with Erica Heilman's niece of the same age, and would have supper there. "The alarm thing is definitely a kind of problem-solving to me. That's just how my mind works."

"Yes, but now that I think about it, it's been for Lizzy's whole lifetime that the alarm's been a problem. It's gone off twice this month already, Zach."

"True enough."

"We don't want to give our daughter the sense that the house she lives in is in a constant state of—"

"Alarm?"

"Yes. Precisely."

"I don't want that either."

"Let's have a séance. You, me, Kazumi, Ardith—not Lizzy, too scary. Lorca, of course."

"Why 'of course' Lorca?"

"Kind of obvious, isn't it, Zach?"

"So you think your so-called ghost is Simon Inescort? You have to be kidding, right?"

"Sort of kidding. Not entirely kidding."

"Come on, Murr."

"And it's not *my* 'so-called ghost.' If it's anything, it's *ours.* I keep coming back to thinking there was probably a very solid reason for a ghost clause in the first place."

"The ghost clause was part of the normal way of thinking and believing back then."

"I like what Faulkner said: the past isn't even past. Maybe we should update our understanding of the ghost clause. Maybe we should consider it 'normal.' Tonight. In the very house we now live in."

"That's all a little too literary."

"No, no, no. Because, first, my sense of what's possible in

the world, Zach, does not derive only from books. So please don't accuse me of that. I think you're accusing me of that. As for being convinced by what ghost stories I've read, nothing comes to mind. All right, with the possible exception of 'The Middle Toe of the Right Foot,' that story by Ambrose Bierce, which always scares the bejesus out of me."

"There's no ghost in our house."

"Zach, try and consider that I might notice different things than you notice."

"I have no doubt of that."

"So, then, let me ask you something. Did you prune the crabapple trees?"

"What are you talking about?"

"Simple question. Did you prune back the crabapple trees?"

"I wouldn't know how."

"Because up by the cabin, the crabapple trees look like they've all just got a haircut or something. Each and every one, clip clip clip, and there's a big garbage bag full of the clippings."

"That has to be Lorca's doing. Remember, she said she'd see to taking care of the cemetery, so probably she meant the trees, too."

"I had the exact same thought, Zach. So I called Lorca up and asked her if she'd pruned the trees or hired someone to prune them, and guess what she said? She said no, she had not. So how did the crabapple trees get trimmed back, Zachary?"

The fact that it was indeed I who had pruned the crabapple trees, and stupidly left the bag full of twig ends and bark scrapings and dead leaves in a garbage bag, just then made me realize that I'd done a very reckless thing. But until that moment, I had no memory of doing it. There's a mental condition I once heard about, called transient amnesia, so maybe I had experienced a temporary memory lapse about the crabapple trees. The thing is, I no longer sleep, and in my condition, maybe I am still somehow affected by sleeplessness. You know, in a normal day-to-day existence, if you have one or two sleepless nights in a row, you are liable to begin making little mistakes, due to absent-mindedness or distraction. Out of exhaustion, your mental gyroscope might, as if touched by a breeze, spin a little off-kilter. You might suddenly forget the streets you navigate home from the pharmacy in town. Or you can't find your wallet. Or you've been out shopping, and you step into your house and put the carton of lemon sorbet in the vegetable bin of the fridge. Or at dinner in a restaurant, you call your dearest friend of thirty-five years by the wrong name. Or you say, "Oh, look at that beautiful sunrise," when you are gazing at a sunset. I may well be grasping at straws here.

Anyway, the sequence of incidents and their consequences I'm now about to describe changed everything for everyone. And so here is what happened.

"Come with me," Zachary said. "I've got to see this for myself." He stood up and took Muriel by the hand and they walked up to the crabapple trees in the dusky light. A week earlier, based on a raise Muriel had received when she got the teaching award, they had finally arranged to transform the cabin into a guest house. The carpenters had been arriving at 7 a.m. and would leave by 4. Lorca had removed all of my books, files, and manuscripts, and the Canadian school desk, too. On the day Muriel and Zachary walked over to look at the crabapple trees, the carpenters had begun to install a small bathroom. They still had a bedroom loft to construct as well.

Since my death, Lorca had planted eight additional crabapple trees. As Muriel stood on the cabin steps, Zachary inspected the trees one by one. He then stood back and took in the entire orchard. He opened the thirty-gallon garbage bag and emptied its contents out on the ground, then sifted through the cuttings.

"Want me to run to the house and get your Sherlock Holmes magnifying glass?" Muriel asked.

Zachary smiled but didn't laugh. Muriel noticed the difference and said, "Zach, it's twigs and scrapings from the trees, like I said. Nobody accidentally left a wristwatch. What, you're going to dust the dry leaves for fingerprints? Come on, Zachary, somebody expertly pruned back the crabapples, and that's that."

"Muriel, I'm not happy with this. It's obviously trespassing of some sort."

"So you think someone *trespassed?* Why? So they could prune these trees?"

"Okay—but maybe one of the carpenters. Carpenters like things neat and clean and in their own place, right? Maybe one of them took care of these trees, to put that kind of order into his working environment or something."

"Why don't you interview them?"

The look Zachary gave Muriel made her realize she should just leave him there and go back to the house, which is what she did. I went along with her.

Zachary stayed up near the trees until dark. By the time he walked back to the house, Muriel had cleared the dishes, rinsed them, and placed them in the dishwasher. She had put the tablecloth in the washing machine for tomorrow's laundry. She had sat at her desk in the library and, in steady short strokes, brushed Epilogue, who, eyes closed, purring, was sitting on her typewriter. She then opened a box from her publisher and read the instructions for signing twenty advance copies, to be sent to bookstore owners, especially on the East Coast. The cover had the title, *Parentheses,* in charcoal letters set between white parentheses. The subtitle, *Erotic Poems of the Japanese Modernist Murei Korin*—a subtitle Muriel had protested—and *Muriel Streuth,* written in off-white cursive, were set against the background of a print from about 1750, *A Girl Drawing Bamboo, While Another Girl Watches,* by Suzuki Harunobu—the cover art was Kazumi's suggestion.

I watched as Muriel signed her author's copy: *To my great love and husband, Zachary—let's consider every room of our farmhouse to be between parentheses. Love, Muriel.* She went upstairs and placed the book under the pillow on Zachary's side of their bed. Then she changed her mind and placed the book on top of his pillow.

Erica brought Elizabeth home, and Muriel put her to bed and read her three children's books, and when the reading was over, she switched on the cat-face night-light and left the door partly open, as always. But Muriel's placement of her own book proved of no consequence, as Zachary kept entirely to his office—which, since Elizabeth was born, had also been the laundry room; he filed and studied his reports next to the washer and dryer and large woven laundry baskets. He had a small table in there, and the gooseneck lamp, bulletin board, and a small file cabinet. Reciprocally, Muriel did not go downstairs and try to talk about anything even partway through. I had no way of telling all of what was going on here; maybe it was just Zachary's brooding over the exchange at the orchard. Yet whatever was the trouble, it kept him awake until roughly 5 a.m., when he fell asleep, head down on his desk. Epilogue was dozing atop the dryer.

The next morning at 7:15, Zachary fed Epilogue, and with mug of coffee in hand, he walked up to the cabin. There were two pickup trucks parked across the road from the farmhouse. The carpenters were Thomas Absher, Wolcott Springhaven, and Wolcott's wife, Sarah. They each had a tool belt on. Wolcott and Sarah were fitting in a sink and bathtub, while Thomas worked from a ladder on the loft. When Zachary said, "Everything looks great here," the carpenters immediately stepped outside to talk with him.

"It's all coming right along," Wolcott said.

"Yeah, I think our time frame—two more weeks— looks pretty good," Sarah said. "Of course, when it comes to the calendar, why believe carpenters, huh?"

"Hope you don't mind me interrupting," Zachary said, "but there's something I'm curious about."

"Fire away," Wolcott said.

They were all standing about five yards from the nearest crabapple tree. Zachary turned to his side and swept his right arm toward the small orchard. "As you might've noticed, these trees have recently been trimmed. And there's a garbage bag filled with twigs and dead leaves and bark."

"Oh, yes," Sarah said. "That would've been four days ago —last Sunday."

"Why do you say that?" Zachary said.

Sarah shrugged. "Had to be."

"And why's that?" Zachary said.

"Because last Saturday they were ragged and unkempt as could be. I think I remember even commenting on it. Do you remember me commenting on that, Wolcott?"

"I remember you used the words 'such negligence,'" Wolcott said.

"Well, that cat's out of the bag, I guess. Sorry, Mr. Anders."

"So, then, I guess you're saying that last Monday you noticed the trees were all nicely trimmed."

"Yes," said Sarah. "Saturday they weren't. Monday they were."

"What did you think about that?" Zachary asked.

"You're a private investigator, aren't you, Mr. Anders?"

"Yes, I am," Zachary said.

All three of the carpenters laughed a little in unison, and Sarah said, "Your bedside manner's a little rusty, I'd say."

"You're right, I'm sorry," Zachary said. "I just can't for the life of me figure out how these crabapples got pruned back like that."

"My guess is, the answer to that will show up in your wife's checkbook," Wolcott said. "I don't want to presume, but I heard younger couples often keep separate checkbooks."

"Sorry to have interrupted your work," Zachary said.

"It won't affect when we take our midmorning break," Thomas said. "You want to take a closer look at anything?"

"No, no," Zachary said. "It all looks great. Thank you."

"Oh, by the way," Sarah said. She held up a box of thirty-gallon garbage bags. "We use a different brand than that garbage bag you pointed out."

I followed Zachary back to the house. Muriel was sitting at the kitchen table with Lizzy. They each were eating a bowl of Cheerios with slices of banana. When Zachary stepped into the kitchen, he saw that Elizabeth was dressed in pajamas with feet on them.

Zachary kissed Lizzy, nuzzled her, and said, "My sweet girl."

"Maybe you haven't actually put pen to paper yet," Muriel said, "but mentally you've started a file on those carpenters, haven't you?"

"Muriel, you're right, it wasn't any of the carpenters, but it wasn't a ghost, either. I apologize for the carpenters, but won't for the ghost."

"What ghost?" Elizabeth asked.

Muriel shot Zachary a dubious look, and he picked Lizzy up, hugged her, swirled her around, and said, "Ooooooo — ooooh — oooh, Daddy is Casper the Friendly Ghost" — Lizzy had watched that cartoon. But now she began to howl with tears, "I don't want you to be a ghost, Daddy. I want you to be Zachary the Friendly Daddy!" She was inconsolable.

Breakfast had suddenly come to a painful point. You sometimes needed to step away from your own haplessness, and Zachary had no idea what to do except to hand Lizzy to her mother and go upstairs and get dressed for work. I'd heard him tell Muriel that his present assignment was to track down a tree surgeon who formerly lived in Middlesex and who had failed to appear in court; he was being sued by his ex-wife, because he had spitefully cut down her stand of three ten-foot pine trees, right after the divorce settlement had left him with about forty dollars in his bank account. Zachary had found out from the tree surgeon's assistant the names, addresses, and times of all of the week's appointments, and he'd no doubt start staking them out in chronological order.

When he returned home around six o'clock, Zachary found a note on the kitchen table: *Zachary, there's a quiche in the fridge. I took Lizzy to see the 5:00 penguin movie — we might stop on the way home and have them heat up some macaroni and cheese for us at the co-op, just for a girls' night out. Co-op's open till eight tonight. I bet you did some interesting research today, huh? Love, Murr and Lizzy.*

How well she knew him! He ate two pieces of cold quiche and then went into his office, where he recorded his day's endeavors and accomplishments. I knew he would eventually edit out the subjective parts for his official report.

"May 2, 1998. I waited in front of 78 Liberty Street, Montpelier — got there about 9:15. The skip, Mr. Barrett Raskins — most recent known residence was 409 Barre Street, Montpelier, but whose present residence is unknown — Raskins, who skipped out on four court appearances, showed up for his 9:45 tree surgeon appointment with a Mrs. Henrietta Coles — she had a lightning-struck oak tree out front that Raskins was supposed to perform surgery on. Raskins stepped out of his truck and walked over to take a look at the tree. At that point, I walked up to him, showed him my identification, and told him he had to wait in his truck while I contacted the police, who would soon be there to take him to jail. He didn't make a fuss. He said—I quote—'Can you wait for me to finish the work on this tree? I'm gonna need all the cash I can get, considering my future.'

"I realize now I should have been more professional, but what I said was 'If you can get the surgery done before the police get here, help yourself.' But it took less than fifteen minutes for me to ask to use Mrs. Coles's telephone and two police officers to arrive. Raskins didn't even have time to complete his examination, let alone balance his ladder against the tree. Anyway, except for routine office work, my day's work was pretty much done by 10:30 a.m.

"Eventually, I'll have to somehow officially make excuses at the agency—I'll think of something—but much of the rest of the day was spent at various nurseries and at places that specialize in planting or removing trees, such as Tree Works, there on Granite Shed Road in Montpelier. All in all, I went to eight different places and talked to at least twenty different people: 'Did you do any work at a house on Peck Hill Road in East Calais lately?' That basic question. Everyone, without exception, went right to their ledgers—nothing, nothing, nothing. My last stop of the day was at Cabot Greenhouse, run by Gary and Vicky, two of the best in the business by any account. Gary can be a curmudgeon, I'd heard on my rounds, but he wasn't anything but helpful, and his wife, Vicky, offered me green tea ice cream, which I accepted, with a cup of tea.

"Here's why I mention Gary and Vicky. It's because of a

word Muriel said when she was teasing me, after we went to look at the crabapple trees up by the cabin. She said, 'Come on, Zachary, somebody expertly pruned back the crabapples, and that's that.' Expertly — that word flew into my head while I was speaking with Vicky and Gary. I asked Gary if he'd ever planted any trees for Simon Inescort. 'I sure did,' Gary said right away. 'Japanese crabapples. Up by his writing cabin. Did you know Simon and Lorca?' I told him that Muriel, Elizabeth, and I lived in Simon and Lorca's former house. 'Oh, yes, I heard someone bought their house,' Vicky said. Then I asked Gary if Simon Inescort knew anything about pruning trees, and Gary said, 'He and I worked together in the spring on those crabapples for two, maybe three years running, and by then he knew everything I did about taking care of them, so I stopped going up there. One summer, when I had a big pruning job — apple trees — I actually called Simon up and asked for his help, and we worked on that, over in Danville, for three straight days. Long hours, too. Simon wasn't a very mechanical guy. He wasn't a Mr. Fixit — he mainly typed. But he had a lot invested in those crabapple trees, so he became a kind of expert with them.'

"Driving home, I thought to myself, We might have a ghost."

OVER THE NEXT FEW DAYS, Zachary didn't say anything of this to Muriel, not that I heard, at least, though I was hardly with them all the time. Off to morning day care at Calais Elementary, or at some playdate or other, Elizabeth was chauffeured around by Muriel.

A book party for Muriel's *Parentheses* was to take place at the farmhouse at the end of the first week in May. Kazumi and Ardith arrived and took up their usual residence in the guest room, across the hall from Elizabeth's room. They brought a case of champagne.

That evening, once Elizabeth was asleep, they caught Muriel up on end-of-the-semester gossip from the University of New Hampshire and the latest of their attempts, ongoing for the second year, to find a country to get married in. "Otherwise, day to day, things are great with us," Kazumi said. "We're very excited about your book."

"It's great that you drove up for the party," Muriel said.

"Everything okay?" Kazumi asked. "You look a little glum."

"Just tired, but fine. Lizzy's had a cold."

"We'll be the waitstaff tomorrow, not to worry," Ardith said.

"There's only going to be ten or twelve people," Muriel said.

"Your esteemed department chair Dr. Bailey included," Ardith said.

"That's really something," Kazumi said, "that she'd drive all the way up."

From his cramped office in the laundry room, Zachary heard them talking late into the night. He had finally written up a full professional report on the fugitive tree surgeon, and then turned to the preliminary file on his next assignment—I saw it on his desk—which had to do with the attempted bribe of an officer at the US Customs and Border Protection crossing, Highgate Springs port of entry. Apparently this guy, whose name is Harry Focable, had a small crate in the trunk of his car filled with what is commonly termed "unlicensed pain medication," which he claimed was for his Canadian cousin, who couldn't afford the drug for his chronic condition. The moment Mr. Focable saw the customs officer reach for his sidearm, he spun his car out of line, tore away south, and disappeared off Route 89 somewhere. Zachary was supposed to pick things up from that point.

While he was working on the preliminaries of that case, he decided to do some laundry.

When the washer loudly took in water and started its cycle, Kazumi said, "It's one in the morning—is Zach in there doing his wash?"

Muriel, who'd had three glasses of Sauvignon Blanc, said, "I sure hope it's Zach."

"What can that possibly mean?" Kazumi said.

"Nothing," Muriel said. "Bad joke."

"Hey, you know what?" Ardith said. "When I went up to check out the progress on our guest house—see, I call it *ours*—obnoxious of me. When I was up there, I noticed the crabapple trees were all tidied up. They look so pretty. Is there such a thing as crabapple jam? Or crabapple pie?"

"Why wouldn't there be?" Kazumi said.

"Too sour or something, maybe," Ardith said.

"Good idea," said Muriel. "I might try making some crabapple jam."

"Who else might be in there doing the wash?" Ardith said.

"Well, we've got this ghost living here. Recently discovered," Muriel said, slightly slurring her words, sipping a fourth glass of wine.

"Is 'ghost' euphemistic for something?" Kazumi asked.

"Yes, it's euphemistic for 'we definitely have a goddamn ghost in our house,'" Muriel said.

"Our celebrated new author's had a little too much Sauvignon Blanc, I fear," Ardith said.

"You're right," Muriel said. "I'm going upstairs now."

THEY ALL THREE LEFT their wineglasses on the dining room table and went upstairs. Epilogue was waiting for Kazumi and Ardith on the guest room bed. "There's the little harlot," Ardith said. She stroked the cat's back and said, "Eppy Eppy Eppy, did you miss us?"

My guess is that Zachary didn't think Muriel would still be awake when he came to the bedroom, but she was. "Zachary, darling, I have a simple yes-or-no question for you."

"You've had a lot of wine."

"Yes or no — do you think we have a ghost?"

Zachary looked caught out. He went into the bathroom, washed his face, brushed his teeth, took off his clothes, and put his bathrobe on. He stood for a moment holding on to a bedpost and looked out the back window at a vast black sky full of stars. Then he said, "Yes."

"Because this has kept us apart," Muriel said.

"A ghost simply can't be true," he said, "but I can't come up with another explanation."

Then, as if suddenly completely sobered up and focused on the opportunity to share what she'd been wanting to share for weeks, if not months, Muriel listed the things she'd experienced. "Zach, our ghost is benevolent, and remember, the word 'benevolent' is not mentioned in the ghost clause framed on the library wall. So not to worry, we aren't going to need to ask Lorca to buy back the house."

"Come on, Murr, it's probably no longer even a legal document."

"Legal document or not has nothing to do with it, does it? Because Lorca would honor it no matter what. I did not believe in ghosts, Zach. I never thought I would. But now I do. And to tell you the truth, I think it's Simon Inescort. And here's why. First, there's the expertly trimmed crabapple trees—before you say anything, Zach, let me tell you that I happened to call Gary and Vicky Katz over at the Cabot Greenhouse. Because I felt it'd be a good thing for us to add to the orchard, so I ordered three more crabapples, and I've told Lorca I did, and she was so pleased. And guess what? Gary told me he told you that Simon Inescort expertly knew how to prune the crabapple trees. So, you had that information, and you didn't tell me you had it, which I understand why you wouldn't, but still, you kept that from me. But here's something else—several something elses. Okay, first. Let me ask you something. Have you ever in your entire life read a novel by Thomas Hardy?"

"The answer to that is no."

"That's not a judgment, Zach. I'm asking for a reason. Which is that three times in the last month, I've found a Thomas Hardy novel—two different ones—facedown on the library floor. I can guarantee you that I personally have not been reading them."

"Fallen from the shelves."

"Open facedown? Every time, open facedown? Plus, my Thomas Hardy hardcovers are on the *bottom* shelf, to the right when you walk in the door."

"So, according to your theory, Simon Inescort is reading Thomas Hardy novels."

"I managed to ask Lorca if her husband——"

"Just tell me."

"Lorca said he had started to read Thomas Hardy again in the weeks before he died."

"Strange coincidence is all."

"Zach, you know what a stickler I am for alphabetizing my books, right?"

"Obsessive, yes."

"Go into the library and look at the bottom shelf, lower right as you walk in the door."

So Zachary did that. When he came back upstairs and into their bedroom, he said, "Left to right, *Tess of the d'Urbervilles* is before *Far from the Madding Crowd.*"

"Which tells you what?"

Zachary, in the half-light of the bedroom, stood at the end of the bed, slowly nodding his head. A few moments went by.

"Zach, finally. Now that we agree we have a ghost, can we sleep together like husband and wife again?"

BUT ONE THING Muriel and Zachary did not yet know was that this very morning, one of the carpenters, Thomas, found my stash of four Moleskine notebooks under the cabin's slat floor. I was standing right there. He looked through one of them briefly, then said, "Hey, look at these. Notebooks or diaries of some sort."

"Let me see those," Sarah said, and glanced through a few pages. "These have to belong to Simon Inescort. This was his writing cabin, you know. Hiding them under the floor— wow, that's what I call privacy."

"Well, look," Thomas said, "since these belonged to Simon, they obviously now belong to his widow, Lorca Pell, right? I drive home past the co-op in Adamant. She lives in the upstairs rooms. I'll drop these notebooks off to her after we get done here today."

"Good deal," Sarah said.

And that was that. They went back to work on the loft and bathroom. I thought of somehow filching my own notebooks, but Thomas had set them under his lunch pail, next to his toolbox—what was I to do? An hour or so later, Thomas drove off with the notebooks on his front seat. I assumed that Lorca would have them in her possession quite soon after.

THE BOOK PARTY WENT very well, up until near the end. Elizabeth was at Erica's niece's house for a sleepover. Kazumi, Ardith, Lorca, and department chair Dr. Bailey were all in attendance, as were Jody and David from up the road, Erica from next door, and a fellow named Michael Witte, who was Muriel's editor at Oxford University Press, who had driven up from New York City and was staying, as was Dr. Bailey, at the Inn at Montpelier. Rick and Andrea, from the Savoy Theater, were also there, as were two local glass artists, Lance and Viiu. Zachary teased Muriel in the kitchen, "Half literary types, half regular people."

"Don't forget to add Simon Inescort to the first category," she said, and walked over to talk to her editor.

Everyone had arrived by 5:30 p.m., plenty of daylight left, the temperature around fifty. The carpenters had worked until 5:00, and Muriel had sent them home with slices of her poppyseed cake. Kazumi, Ardith, and Muriel had prepared a salad in a big wooden bowl, sesame chicken and rice, and an enormous fillet of salmon seasoned with lemon pepper. There were platters of asparagus. Lorca had contributed two loaves of bread and five bottles of white wine, which she brought already chilled.

With plates in hand, people congregated in the living room and dining room. Ardith was in charge of the old vinyl albums of Miles Davis, Keith Jarrett, and others to be played on the phonograph. After a couple of hours of eating, serious and unserious talk, the two poppyseed cakes (one with the carpenter's portions missing) that Muriel had baked were set on the dining room table, along with lemon sorbet and dessert plates. Zachary hurriedly filled new glasses with champagne and distributed them, keeping one for himself, of course. Michael Witte tapped his glass with a spoon, the rooms quieted down, and he said, "If I may, I'd like to propose a toast." He raised his glass. "In my eighteen years there, I've never been prouder to be an editor at Oxford University Press than this evening. Not only because Dr. Muriel

Streuth is on our list, but most of all, that with *Parentheses* she has written a truly original and intellectually—and I might add emotionally—provocative book."

Glasses were raised and champagne was drunk. Muriel kissed Michael on the cheek, kissed Zachary on the mouth, and made her way to the front window, through which the maples could be seen. Michael tapped his glass again, everyone listened up, and Muriel said, "My darling husband, Zach, has suffered through every draft of my book—"

"The poems are very enjoyable," Zachary said, himself a little tipsy, and laughter rolled through the room.

"As for the translations of Korin's poems themselves," Muriel said, "I have only Kazumi Tanaka to thank for those. So, Kazumi, thank you. And thank you, Michael, for your brilliant editing. Now, the thing about Kazumi is, she's incorrigible—and she insisted that I read one of Mukei Korin's poems found in my book."

There was applause, and Erica said, "From what I've heard, we might need a fire extinguisher!"

I went into the library. And at this point I heard a loud clattering, because a cat Epilogue's size can make quite a ruckus flinging himself up against a bookshelf. Epilogue landed on the floor, then leapt up onto the rocking chair, where he stared toward where I stood near the doorway.

"Oh, that's just our resident catamount, Eppy," Muriel said.

When Kazumi handed Muriel a copy of her book, she saw that Kazumi had inserted a bookmark. Muriel opened the book at that page and began reading:

A rowboat floats oarless on a pond.
Bow to stern, a cat paces the rim.
Her personal history has proven
that on moonlit nights
her balance is never doubtful.

"Now, here's the lines inside the parentheses," Muriel said, and continued to read:

(my tongue on your breast, yours tasting the palm of my hand; our
configurations of night-love have varied for hours — what if the
moon never leaves the sky?)

When Kazumi said, "End parentheses," the MOTION IN LIBRARY alarm went off. Apart from the harsh beeping interruption, it almost made for a slapstick moment. I now stood at the bottom of the stairs and could see into the living room. "The phone's about to ring," Muriel said. "Zachary?"

Indeed, the wall telephone in the kitchen rang as Zachary was walking toward it. He picked up and said, "This is Zachary Anders — we have a house full of people. The MOTION IN LIBRARY went off and nobody but the cat's in the library." He hung up.

Muriel had by this time pressed the OFF code and returned to her guests. "Very sorry," she said. "Our ghost sets off the alarm, you see."

This, of course, drew chuckles and exaggerated frowns of dubious sympathy. "Oh, well, you heard the best lines of the poem, anyway!" Now everyone moved to the dining room table for their poppyseed cake and sorbet. Near the front hallway, Ardith said to Muriel, "There's a full moon tonight, in case you didn't realize. Considering that poem you read, it might bode well for *urgent agreement* later on — maybe you and Zach will agree all night."

"How much champagne have you had?" Muriel said.

"Not nearly enough," Ardith said.

All the guests were gone by 10:45. Kazumi and Ardith announced that they were staying at a B&B in town instead of in the guest room. "I called on the library phone, and there's plenty of vacancies."

"Why waste the money?" Muriel asked.

"Oh, it's very reasonable, Betsy's B&B," Kazumi said. "And besides, we think you've had enough company for tonight. Let's all have dinner tomorrow, and me and Ardith will move right back in."

"I think you're erring on the generous side," Muriel said. "But have fun in town."

"We'll leave our suitcases here, okay?" Kazumi said.

"Of course," Muriel said.

Kazumi and Ardith grabbed a few toiletries and changes of clothes, fit everything into a large handbag, and off they went to Montpelier, driving away under a full moon flooding the fields and hills and trees and back roads.

Muriel waited in bed for Zachary. When he stepped from the shower, he put on his bathrobe and sat on the end of the bed. "I can't wait to feel you inside me, Zach," Muriel said.

"Can you at least wait till I get into the bed with you?"

This not only made Muriel laugh, but seemed to relax her, too, and when they began to kiss, I went out to my cabin —

it was as if I was the first overnight guest there. The loft was nearly completed. I lay in what would be the bedroom and looked out the large window at the thistle field and stone wall in the moonlight.

Two days later, Monday, around 6 p.m., Kazumi and Ardith left for New Hampshire. Zachary had called to say he would be working late.

Muriel and Elizabeth were turning over soil in the garden. Lizzy had her gardening outfit on: overalls, a flannel shirt, socks, and tennis shoes. Her hair frizzed out from under a floppy hat. She held a plastic trowel.

Elizabeth was helping her mother plant sunflowers along the stone wall, one of the flowers they planted in early spring. Just when Muriel said, "Sweetheart, Mommy's going in to make dinner, but I can see you out the kitchen window, so you wave at me, okay? You're doing a great job. Our sunflowers are going to be big and beautiful," Lorca drove up and parked across from the farmhouse.

"You know Auntie Lorca's going to stay with you this evening, remember?"

Over the past month or so, Elizabeth had begun to call Lorca "Auntie Lorca," and now she ran toward Lorca, who'd walked from her car to the lawn. Lorca was carrying a brown Dutch schoolbag. "Hello, sweet pea," she said, hugging Lizzy and turning in a circle. "Did you plant that very big tree there?" Lorca pointed to an enormous butternut at the end of the stone wall, where it met the road.

"No, silly," Lizzy said. "God planted that tree. I only plant tomatoes and sunflowers."

Hand in hand, they walked into the house, where Muriel had finished preparing a salade Niçoise for herself and Lorca, and a grilled cheese and tomato sandwich, cut into six squares, for Lizzy.

Elizabeth took a toothpick and removed the very little dirt from under her fingernails, which she sprinkled into a planter on the kitchen sill, which contained an early sprouting of mint. All that completed, Lizzy went into the bathroom and washed her hands, then sat at the kitchen table with Lorca and Muriel.

"You did such a good job planting that big butternut tree!" Lorca said.

"Nooooooooooo, nooooo, noooo, that tree was already there when I was born!" Lizzy said, laughing.

"Are you sure about that?" Lorca said.

"Yeeeeeeeeeees," Elizabeth said, taking up her first square of sandwich.

"Did you see any rabbits or woodchucks out in the garden today, sweet pea?" Lorca asked.

"Mommy says I have to shout and chase them away," Elizabeth said.

"Only until the lilies grow to full size," Muriel said. To Lorca she said, "Then there's the deer."

"It's nearly time for hummingbird feeders to be put out, too, isn't it?" Lorca said. "Not quite time, but almost."

They ate and talked, and Muriel said, "I see you brought a schoolbag with you."

"Yeah, I brought sketchbooks along this evening," Lorca said.

"Did you have fun at the party?" Muriel asked.

"A great deal of fun. I had to have two espressos before

driving back to Adamant," Lorca said. "Did you think it was a success?"

"People stayed kind of late, for Vermont. That's a good sign, right?"

After clearing the dishes, Muriel said, "I'll be at the Savoy from six-thirty to eight, then at Sarducci's with Zach. I imagine we'll get back by ten, latest. Thank you for staying with Lizzy."

"I brought a new book to see if you like it, sweet pea," Lorca said.

"Elizabeth, remember, just one Buster Keaton movie, then three books, then right to bed, okay?"

"One movie, three books, and a movie," Elizabeth said.

"What do you think, Auntie Lorca?"

"I think one book, then a Buster Keaton movie, then two more books," Lorca said. "How about that?"

Elizabeth thought for a moment and said, "I think a million movies and a million books!"

"It's a deal," Lorca said.

Something had been worked out there. Muriel hugged and kissed Elizabeth, walked out to her car, and drove down the road.

Elizabeth was fast asleep by 8:30. Lorca sat on the rocking chair in the library. She hadn't mentioned receiving my notebooks, but was now reading them by the light of the floor lamp. Epilogue was on the typewriter. She read for about forty-five minutes, then looked up when Epilogue dropped to the floor, crouched, and padded forward in slow motion, in full stalking mode, toward where I was standing in the room, at the farthest point from the desk. It was then that I made a decision, whether reckless or not, because I felt it was time. I reached up, pulled out *The Collected Poems of Wallace Stevens,* and let the book drop to the floor. Epilogue immediately pounced on the book, scratched once at the cover, then hightailed it out of the library.

The room was silent for a good five minutes, during which Lorca, notebook on her lap, hand on her heart, stared at the now-empty slot on the bookshelf, and then lower. Finally, she closed her eyes and said, "Simon, I miss you very much. If you're not here, then no matter, I'm only talking to myself. But if you are here, I need to tell you something.

"When we lived in this house together, we had the photographs of our ancestors in the front hall. And right in the middle, we had a small oval mirror in an antique frame, remember? And every now and then I'd see you standing there, looking into that small mirror. This moment always kind of disturbed me. The reason was, by standing there looking in the mirror, you were in essence adding your portrait to the others. It was as if you were auditioning for your own passing. It always used to freak me out.

"And now I've read your notebooks. The ones Thomas told me he found under the slats in your cabin. Reading through them, I at first wanted to think, Okay, this is part of a novel Simon was working on before he died. But of course, how could that be? Because how could you use the names Muriel and Zachary—and Elizabeth? Cruel trick of my imagination, I wanted to think, cruel trick. I am going crazy —bereavement has made me completely nuts. What can I be reading here in these notebooks? In your handwriting. You cannot exist and yet you exist? I may well now require a psychiatrist twice a day for the rest of my life — certainly I require a brain scan and medications. What is it I require, Simon? Still, I confess that I believe what I am experiencing and am not afraid of it.

"I'm not afraid of you, my darling. So, if you are here, if you are listening, this is what I need to say.

"I want you to come live with me. When Muriel and Zachary get back tonight, and I walk out to my car, I want you to be sitting on the passenger side.

"But right now — right this minute, Simon — I'm going outside, onto the lawn. And I'm going to burn these notebooks. Because you have to stop this. I read where you have some notion of Muriel and Zachary finding them someday and discovering who they were. If that should happen, do you know what it would mean? It would mean that they would realize they had been observed. How could they possibly comprehend that? Why burden them with that? What you filled these notebooks with, Simon, are your memories, not theirs. Your writing about their marriage can't complete the years taken from your and my marriage. You must stop this. I will never forgive you if you don't stop this. I love you. But please stop. You need to let this young family have their own lives."

Lorca carried the notebooks and a section of the *Times Argus* out to an area near the garden along the stone wall. She took out a small box of matches from her jeans pocket. She set the notebooks, each opened to its middle pages, on top of the newspaper. She struck a match and lit the corner of a page. Quickly the paper flared, and in about fifteen minutes all but the leather bindings were gone — ashes floated up and away like black moths. When Lorca looked back toward the house, she saw Elizabeth standing behind the lace curtain of the guest room, watching everything. Epilogue was on the sill of the same window.

Lorca went back inside the house, and into the library. She sat looking out toward the maple trees, alternately weeping and laughing a little, saying, "How can I still be so angry at you? Maybe it's just because you died. I don't know."

It was then I performed the final reckless act. I typed on a piece of paper Muriel had left in the manual typewriter:

I will wait in the car.

Lorca inhaled sharply, ran into the bathroom, stuck her mouth under the spigot, and took great gulps of water. Back in the library, she peeled the paper from the typewriter and folded it into her back pocket. She then went up and lay on the floor of Elizabeth's room. Elizabeth was back in bed.

"Why did you start a fire by the garden?" Elizabeth asked. "Was it like the girl in that story you read me? She thought a campfire was a way of talking to the stars."

"Yes, that's why," Lorca said.

"Okay," Elizabeth said. "Night-night."

IT WASN'T UNTIL WE had reached Adamant Road that Lorca said, "I don't want you typing out any more notes for me. Simon, please, no more notes. It'd be too much for me. And when you finally are gone—if that's the way it works. If that's the way it works, when you are finally gone, I will either know right away or know it later, but I will know it. Of that I'm quite certain. In the meantime, every day, all day, I'll think of us as living together at the shortest distance between two worlds."

Lorca drove slowly, and five minutes from the co-op she simply stopped the car under a canopy of oak trees. She turned on the classical music program. Couperin's *Les Barricades mystérieuses* was playing, one of her favorites. We were both weeping now. She turned up the volume slightly. She looked out her side window. I can only imagine what was borne up on her tears. But for me there was an overpowering tactile sensation, which I believe was the salt spray from those dolphins against my face. For the briefest moment in the ocean I had woken to their passing.

The author is grateful to Melanie Jackson, Deanne Urmy, David Wyatt, and Tom Absher for their close reading and encouragement.